THE VIEW FROM THE CHERRY TREE

THE VIEW FROM THE CHERRY TREE

BY WILLO DAVIS ROBERTS

Aladdin Books
Macmillan Publishing Company
New York

Aladdin Books
Macmillan Publishing Company
866 Third Avenue, New York, NY 10022
Collier Macmillan Canada, Inc.

First Aladdin Books edition 1987

Printed in the United States of America

A hardcover edition of *The View from the Cherry Tree* is
available from Atheneum Publishers, Macmillan Publishing
Company.

20 19 18 17 16 15 14 13 12 11

Library of Congress Cataloging-in-Publication Data

Roberts, Willo Davis.
    The view from the cherry tree.

    Summary: Rob admits having seen a murder, but no one
believes him—except the murderer.
    [1. Mystery and detective stories] I. Title.
PZ7.R54465Vi   1987   [Fic]   86-22233
ISBN 0-689-71131-X (pbk.)

To THE KIDS, who provided
a good deal of the material
in this story

THE VIEW
FROM THE
CHERRY TREE

1

From his perch in the cherry tree Rob Mallory could see into the houses on either side. It was the Mallory's tree, but it was closest to Mrs. Calloway's house; right up against it, as a matter of fact, and one of the numerous causes of problems with their neighbor.

It was into Mrs. Calloway's dining room that he was looking; behind him, at home, female voices came through the open windows. He couldn't understand what they were saying because they were all talking at once, but he knew, anyway. Something about the wedding. All anybody talked about these days was the wedding, like there was a law, or something, that made other subjects forbidden.

The day was warm enough for even Old Lady Calloway to open her windows, and the slight breeze stirred the heavy lace curtains so that he caught glimpses of the inside.

He had lived next door to Mrs. Calloway for nine of his eleven years, but he'd never been inside her house. When he was little, he'd believed the stories

3

the older kids told, about how she caught kids and ate them, like the witch in Hansel and Gretel. Now he didn't believe that anymore, but he wouldn't have gone inside her house for anything.

Mrs. Calloway's rug was dark red, which ought to have been pretty, but it wasn't. He couldn't tell if it was dusty, but he imagined it smelled funny, the way the old lady herself did. The furniture was all old and funny looking, too, very dark and depressing.

As he sat with his back against a big limb, eating cherries and spitting out the pits, he saw S.O.B. creeping across the lawn toward Mrs. Calloway's house.

S.O.B. was twenty-two pounds of the meanest cat in the country. The initials meant just what you'd think they meant. Darcy had named him Sonny, but Dad kept referring to him as "that son-of-a-bitching cat" and pretty soon he was S.O.B.

Rob watched with interest as the cat approached the corner of the Calloway house. Mrs. Calloway hated cats, and Rob was supposed to keep S.O.B. away from her place, but what sense did that make? You couldn't police a cat all the time.

S.O.B. made the leap from lawn to limb in one long bound, sitting below Rob in the cherry tree for a moment, then inching out toward the blowing curtains in Mrs. Calloway's window.

Rob knew perfectly well that he ought to stop him. The old lady would have fits if S.O.B. landed in her dining room. That was his mother's phrase . . . somebody was always "having fits," or about to. He'd never actually seen it happen, and he couldn't think of a better place to see it than with Mrs. Calloway.

4

S.O.B. crouched at the end of the limb, his tail twitching, then still. The muscles bunched under the black pelt as he prepared to attack the curtains. And then Rob missed the action because out front a car horn sounded and he let it distract him for just a second. When he looked back, the curtains were still flapping, but S.O.B. was gone.

He waited, hoping something would happen. Like the old lady would start yelling, and maybe she'd froth at the mouth when she had her fit. That's what dogs did. He'd never seen one, but he'd heard about it.

The car horn was just old Max, and now he was coming around the side of the house toward the back door. You'd think Max would quit coming around all the time, now that Darcy was getting married to Steve.

Old Max was twenty-one, and for a grown-up he wasn't bad. He had a sense of humor, which was more than some of the rest of them had.

Rob threw a cherry pit, but it was too light; it fell short, so he pitched a whole cherry. The second one hit Max between the eyes.

Max paused, looking upward into the tree and stepping off the sidewalk. "That you, Robbie?"

"I'm a frog prince."

"No kidding. You do look sort of green at that, but I thought it was the reflection of the leaves. Where is everybody?"

"If you mean Darcy, she's having something altered. It's an emergency. Everything's an emergency at our house these days."

"Yeah. Okay if I go on in?"

"If it's not, they'll throw you out," Rob said. "That's what happens to me. It's not my fault they run around in their underwear, but they expect me to know when to open a door."

Max considered, nodded, said "Thanks," and rapped on the back screen door before entering the porch. "Anybody home? Are you all decent?"

There was a chorus of voices; his sister Teddi answered the door and let Max in.

Rob waited a little longer for something to happen in the Calloway house, then gave up. Maybe the old lady was taking a nap. She often took a nap, right when people wanted to use their power mowers or play their stereos or something. No matter when you needed to make a noise, she was taking a nap.

He pictured S.O.B. stalking through the odd-smelling house, finding the bedroom, and leaping onto the old lady's chest. That would give her a fit, all right, if twenty-two pounds of cat landed on her!

He'd been eating cherries for half an hour, but he needed more than that. Cherries weren't very filling. He wondered if they were ever going to have dinner. It was time somebody started cooking something if they were.

He slid down as far as he could go and then dropped onto the grass, his tennis shoes making no sound. Going in, he slammed the screen door, expecting someone would say something, but they were all too busy. Rob sighed. Nothing happened the way it was supposed to around here any more.

The kitchen was empty. There wasn't anything cooking, no good smells coming from the oven. He opened the refrigerator door and debated whether it would be worth it to cut a slice off that cold ham. It was all fancied up and they'd be able to tell if he cut it. Usually his mother was fairly reasonable about such things, but these days it was hard to tell. He decided he'd better leave it alone and settle for a peanut butter and jelly sandwich.

The dining room was full of women, but they'd let old Max in, so they must all be dressed. Rob licked the oozing jelly from the edges of his bread and stood in the doorway, looking them over.

His older sister Darcy was the one getting married. You'd think she was a queen, or something, the way everybody waited on her and catered to her. Darcy had dark hair and blue eyes, like Mrs. Mallory, and while she just seemed like old Darcy to him she must be pretty because all these guys kept coming around, even after she was engaged to Steve. She was standing on a chair while her mother pinned a hem in her dress.

"Don't get that on anything, Robbie," Mrs. Mallory said. "And somebody answer that telephone."

Teddi, her long hair swirling as she spun, stretched across Max to reach the instrument on the table near the doorway. Because she was the one moving, Rob looked at her.

Teddi wasn't as pretty as Darcy, but he liked her better. Of course she was closer to his own age, being only six years older, and she didn't look down on him quite as much as the others did.

Teddi picked up the telephone and answered it.

"Yes? Mallory residence. Oh. Yes, Mrs. Calloway." She winced, holding the receiver away from her ear.

"Yes. Yes. Yes, I understand. Yes, I'm sorry. I'm sorry." She looked at her mother, rolling her eyes until Mrs. Mallory rose and offered to take over for her. Teddi shook her head, then mouthed a final "Yes, I'm sorry" before she hung up. "Mrs. Calloway."

"We gathered that. What is it this time?"

"Couple of things. Max is parked on her garden hose. He's ruined it, she says. She'll have to have a new one, and he'll have to pay for it."

Max scowled. "I'm parked at the curb. Where's her crummy hose, in the street?"

Teddi shrugged. "I don't know. Besides that, Mom, S.O.B. got into her house."

A moan sounded through the room. Mrs. Mallory ran a hand over the lower part of her face. "All right. What did he break?"

"He walked across her bed after he'd knocked over a potted plant she'd just watered, and tracked mud all over the spread. Then he ate one of her goldfish. An expensive variety. We owe her for that, too. She spilled the rest of them onto the floor while she was trying to chase him away, and it's no thanks to us that she didn't lose them all."

"Where's S.O.B. now?" Mrs. Mallory's mouth was a flat line as she went back to her task of pinning the hem.

"That's the final part. She threw him out, and he scratched her."

"Well, naturally," Max said. "He's not an idiot, that cat."

"She's going to have to have a tetanus shot, she's sure, and maybe rabies shots."

"S.O.B.'s had his rabies shots," Mrs. Mallory said, jabbing angrily with a pin until Darcy protested. "Rob, I wish you'd find a way to keep that cat away from her."

Rob spoke around the final mouthful of peanut butter and jelly. "I can't watch him all the time. He just doesn't like Mrs. Calloway."

"Nobody likes Mrs. Calloway," Max agreed.

"It's the only thing I don't like about this house," Mrs. Mallory said. "Having her for a neighbor. Don't mention this latest ruckus to your father; he'll have a fit."

Rob tried to imagine his father having a fit and failed. "When are we going to eat?"

"What time is it? That late already? I'm going to have to stop pretty soon, Darcy."

"Not before this is finished, I hope!"

"I've got it pinned, now. You can do the hem yourself while I'm starting dinner."

"No, I can't, Mom. Steve's picking me up in fifteen minutes. We still have to go talk to Mr. Felton about the music. That has to be done tonight, so he knows what to play at the rehearsal tomorrow night."

"Well, take it off, and don't knock any pins out of it, and I'll see what I can do later. That confounded telephone has rung twenty times this afternoon; I'm beginning to want to tear it out of the wall." She answered it herself this time. "Yes, oh, is that you, Vivian? Yes, just a minute, let me get to the other phone."

Max helped Darcy down. "It's a shame, kid, you wasting yourself on that Sanderson bum. After all, you could have had me."

"Sorry, lamb," Darcy said. "Excuse me, I have to run. See you later."

Max let her go, and brought his gaze around to Teddi and smiled. "Dinner's going to be late around here. Why don't we go catch a bite at Dino's?"

Astonishment flashed over her face. "Me?"

Rob watched the byplay with mild interest. Outside the window he saw S.O.B. streaking up the trunk of the cherry tree to vanish into its secret places. He was all right, then. Too bad he'd had his shots; Old Lady Calloway deserved rabies or something.

"Sure, you. Maybe even the frog prince. How about it, your highness?"

Rob shook his head. "No, thanks."

"I'll ask Mom." Teddi grinned and took off for the den and the other telephone where her mother was speaking.

Max sighed. "I wonder how much that old bag thinks her hose was worth?"

"It was an old one," Rob said. "It leaked."

"Did it, now? I wouldn't be surprised if she laid it out where somebody'd have to run over it so she could get herself a new one."

"How old do you have to get before you drop dead of old age?"

Max laughed. "Older than that crone, I'm afraid. Although she's mean enough to poison herself on her own spit. Find me an ashtray, will you, sprout? This place is so cleaned up I don't dare touch anything."

Rob headed for the kitchen. He was reaching for the ashtrays stacked on the counter when he heard his father's footsteps on the back porch. The floor always creaked there under Walt Mallory's two hundred pounds.

Rob liked his father. They didn't talk an awful lot, but he wasn't a grouch like some kids' fathers.

He wore light gray work clothes, sweat-stained under the arms and across the back. He said, "Hiya, chum," and got himself a glass of iced tea out of the refrigerator. "What are we having for dinner?"

"I don't know. Nothing's started yet; they've all been fussing about Darcy's clothes."

"Where's your mother?"

"On the phone." He decided to spill some of the news. "Max parked on Old Lady Calloway's hose, and she says he has to buy her a new one. The one she had was wrecked already."

"She's a winner, that one." Mr. Mallory opened the refrigerator again and poked around. "You suppose it's safe to eat some of this salami?"

"Darcy did. But that's not saying anyone else can. If anybody ever fixes dinner around here, let me know, huh?"

He wandered back through the dining room, to where Max was standing with a handful of ashes, and passed along the ashtray. Max nodded without looking at him. He was busy looking at Teddi.

"What do you mean, you can't go? You're seventeen years old, for crying out loud! You can't go out to a drive-in for a hamburger?"

"It's because of the wedding. Mom's about frantic, there's still so much to do. She wants us all to hang around to help with the loose ends."

11

"Even if you starve?"

"Oh, we'll throw something together." Teddi brightened. "Why don't you stay and eat with us? It won't be anything fancy, but you're welcome."

"I thought you'd never ask. Listen, is it safe to sit down anywhere except on a straight chair in this house?"

"Let's go out on the porch and sit in the swing. It's cooler."

Rob watched them go, then made his way down the hallway toward the front of the house. His mother was still talking on the telephone, sounding harassed, the way she had for the past month.

"There are only two categories things fall into around here now," she was saying. "Things that *have* to be done before the wedding, and things that can't possibly be squeezed in until afterward. I hope when Teddi decides to get married she elopes."

The living room was empty and pleasantly dim with the draperies drawn against the afternoon sun. Rob turned on the television and sprawled in a chair. After a few minutes S.O.B. came strolling through the cat-door from the front porch and leaped into the big recliner, settling down to wash himself.

"I hope you gave it to her good," Rob said. S.O.B. didn't pay any attention.

The doorbell rang. Rob waited, thinking surely someone else would get it. After awhile it rang again, and his mother shouted from the den, "Robbie! Get the door!"

He scuffed his feet through the shag carpeting, taking as long over it as he could. It was Derek Calloway.

12

Rob stared at him through the screen door.

"Well, come on, let me in," Derek suggested.

Rob hunched his shoulders and unlatched the screen. "So come in. There's nobody around. Darcy's gone off someplace with Steve."

"I used to be a friend of the family. I thought." Derek was one of the grown-ups, too; he had been engaged to Darcy once, before Steve came along.

Rob padded back into the living room and flopped in his chair. Derek stood looking at the television for a moment.

"How come you got all their faces green?"

"I like green. I can pretend they're Martians."

"Oh. Is your mother around?"

"She's in the den. On the phone." Rob didn't take his eyes off the screen.

"Teddi?"

"Out in the porch swing. With old Max."

Small lines appeared in Derek's forehead. "Is *he* here?"

"How else could he be in the swing with Teddi?"

Derek sighed. "You don't mind if I go back and get myself a drink of water, do you?"

Rob shrugged. "Go ahead."

As Derek turned to go, S.O.B. dove off the chair in front of him, tangling in Derek's size-twelve shoes. The cat howled and spat. Derek swore and righted himself with an effort.

"Maybe Aunt Bea's right about him. He's a menace."

"He probably thinks the same thing about guys with big feet. You been over there? To her house?"

Derek's Aunt Bea was Mrs. Calloway.

"Yeah. My mother sent her some fresh peas. I hear you're in trouble again."

"Oh? How's that?"

"Cutting across the old gal's lawn again. I should think you'd learn, Rob."

"Oh, that was two days ago. And I didn't cut across on purpose, Hal Stumper ran into me on his bike and knocked me over on her grass. How the heck could I help that?"

"Oh, is that the way it was? She made it sound like you were deliberately making a path across her corner. I should have known." Derek stared glumly at the green faces on TV. He frowned at a jar with a punctured lid that sat atop the television set.

"What's that?"

"My spiders." Rob didn't bother to keep the contempt out of his voice; anybody with one eye could see what was in the jar.

Derek shifted uneasily, moving away from them. "Jeeze, you sure collect the darndest things. How can you stand to touch them?"

That didn't even deserve an answer, so he didn't make one.

"How come they're sitting on the TV?"

"Because my mother said I had to get them out of my bedroom before Uncle Nick gets here. I don't know why. *He* isn't scared of spiders."

"And she told you to put them in the living room?" Derek's dark thick brows rose in disbelief.

"No, she said to get them out of *my* room." He knew perfectly well his mother wouldn't allow them to stay where they were while there was company in the house, but he hadn't yet thought of a safe place to put them. "You wouldn't want to keep them for a few days, would you?"

Derek shuddered. "I'd have nightmares with those things in the same room with me!" He stared a moment longer, then left the room.

Rob's father came in, his hair dark red from being wet, freshly showered and changed into slacks and a sport shirt. "How come you got all their faces green?"

"I like green."

"Well, I don't." Mr. Mallory twiddled with the dials, changing the complexions to magenta and finally to something nearer flesh tones. Then he fished the evening paper out of a stack of magazines on the coffee table. "This place is so neat you can't find anything. The wedding is at the church, the reception is at the Country Club, so why does the house have to be so neat?"

"I don't know. I think I'll go outdoors for a while. It's cooler. Be sure to call me when there's something to eat, okay?"

"Okay," his father agreed. "And for pete's sake stay away from Old Lady Calloway, will you, chum?"

He didn't know why they were always saying that to him. He never went near her on purpose. Never once, that he could remember, in his entire life had he gone near her on purpose.

S.O.B. followed him down the back steps. Maybe, Rob thought, he'd eat a few more cherries, just to keep from starving to death.

He liked it in the cherry tree. It was almost as good

as Old Lady Calloway's tower for keeping track of things. He could see both ways up and down the street, and into both houses, and across the street to the Comptons' and the Devereauxs'.

The tower was a little better, he supposed, although he'd never been in it. It was the one thing about her house that he liked. It was a round tower that went up three stories, but the top ones were closed off. Mrs. Calloway sat at the lower floor level all the time to watch what was going on up and down the street.

The tower opened off one corner of Mrs. Calloway's living room, and it had windows all around it. These were heavily hung with lace curtains so that unless it was night and she had the lights on it was hard to see into it. Mrs. Calloway sat in there during the day with her binoculars, and there wasn't much that happened on Saraday Street that she didn't know about.

S.O.B. didn't join Rob in the tree. He went on out across the lawn to where Max's car was still parked on Old Lady Calloway's hose, and jumped in the window of the car.

"Hey! Get out of there!" Max got up from the porch swing, Teddi following, and they went out toward the street. "Come on, Ess Old Boy, get out of my car. You're too hard on the upholstery."

S.O.B. was perched on the back of the front seat. He laid back his ears as they came up, and twitched his tail.

Max hesitated. "Get him out of there, will you, Teddi?"

"Come on, love. Come out," Teddi coaxed.

S.O.B. crouched lower.

16

"Where's Rob? He can always pick him up without getting scratched. Rob?" Max turned to call.

Rob spat out a pit and picked another cherry. Poor old chicken Max.

It took them a few minutes, but Teddi finally got the cat out, and Max ran up the windows to keep him from going back. While he was doing it, Mrs. Calloway came out onto her front steps and called down to them.

"Young man, your car has ruined my hose!"

She had a loud voice for such a little dried-up person. She looked a lot like the witch from Hansel and Gretel, Rob thought. Only he couldn't imagine her living in a gingerbread house, not a real one.

"You've got it hanging over the edge of the curb into the street," Max pointed out.

"You've ruined it. It's split; I can't use it anymore."

"It leaked before."

Mrs. Calloway advanced down the steps as if to take hold of him. "That's not so. A hose will cost me fifteen dollars. You'll have to pay for it; you can't expect to ruin people's property and not make it good."

"Mrs. Calloway, that hose wasn't worth anywhere near fifteen dollars. A new one wouldn't cost that much, even a better one than you had."

She took a different tack. "Always parking in front of my house, as if you owned the curb. You're visiting the Mallorys, park in front of *their* house."

"There isn't room in front of their house. Nobody ever parks in front of your house, and you don't have a car."

"That is hardly any concern of yours. I'll thank you

17

to move the car and replace my hose, or I'll have the police on you."

Max stared at her for a moment, then touched Teddi's arm. "You do that, Mrs. Calloway. Come on, Teddi, let's go."

S.O.B., still in Teddi's arms, spat at their neighbor when she came too near; the old woman retreated, muttering, and Max and Teddi came back into the yard, under the cherry tree.

"Do you think she'll do it? Call the police?"

Max made an exasperated sound. "Let her. For cripes sake, she doesn't own the street, and even if she had any company, I wouldn't be blocking all the parking! I did run over her crummy hose, after she put it in the gutter where I couldn't help it, so maybe I'll replace it, but I can get one cheaper than that. It's only a twenty-five footer, and it must be fifteen years old!"

"Maybe I'd better go in and see if Mom needs some help. She's about worn out. You want to come in? You're going to stay, aren't you?"

"Sure, I'll stay. Celebrate the end of an era."

"I guess Derek feels the same way. He's here, too; I see him looking out the window."

Rob picked another cherry and concentrated on spitting it as far as Mrs. Calloway's window. He'd never made it, but sometimes he got one as far as the sill.

He'd be glad when this blamed wedding was over, and they got back to normal around here.

2

Sometimes somebody spoke to him. "Rob, haven't you got a clean shirt?" or "Don't mess up the living room." But mostly they didn't notice he was around. When dinner was finally ready, he ate in silence. After dinner the rest of them went off on their own business. Rob stayed out of their way while they were leaving.

S.O.B. wasn't quite so agile, however; he managed to get tangled up with Max's feet, and there was a bit of spitting and swearing for a minute before Rob rescued the cat.

Mr. Mallory paused on his way through the dining room with the evening paper. "Maybe we'd be smart to put that cat in a kennel until the wedding is over."

Rob's arms tightened protectively around S.O.B. "Why should he have to get punished because old Darcy's getting married?"

"I wasn't thinking of it as a punishment, necessarily. More like protective custody. You know, keep him from getting into trouble."

Rob stroked the sleek black fur. "He won't get into trouble. If people'd look where they're stepping, he'd be all right."

His father looked at him for a moment, then sighed. "Well, keep him away from everybody, will you, chum? Including our gracious neighbor, Mrs. Calloway."

"Wally? Have you got a few minutes?" That was his mother.

"I was going to finish reading the paper. What do you need?"

"Well, I thought maybe you could write out the checks for the wedding expenses. I made a list. I have to get that dress hemmed so Darcy can pack it. She'll have a fit if she can't take it with her."

He could see his father didn't really want to write checks. On the other hand, it was easier these days to go ahead and do what Mom wanted than to argue it all out with her, and you still wound up doing it her way in the end, anyway.

"Okay. Where's the list?"

Rob moved out of the way, slipping out the back door before anybody thought up anything they wanted him to do. He was supposed to straighten up his room, and if his mother checked she'd see he still had some stuff around. He'd have plenty of time to do that tomorrow, anyway. He didn't see what difference it made to Uncle Nick (who was to have the other bed in Rob's room for tomorrow night) if there was a little lint under the bed. He'd bet Uncle Nick wouldn't even notice it. Chances were he wouldn't be bothered by a can of worms on the nightstand, either, but his mother never considered that other people's sensibilities weren't the same as hers.

It was a warm summer evening. There ought to be something to do, but he couldn't think of anything. S.O.B. squirmed to get out of his arms, and Rob let him go with a warning.

"You heard what Dad said. Stay out of trouble, cat, or we're both in for it. They might even send you to the pound."

In the light that streamed through the back screen, S.O.B. gave him a malevolent look.

"No, I don't think they'd dare, either," Rob agreed, and hoisted himself into the cherry tree. It was harder to find the ripe cherries in the dark, but not impossible. He could see into the dining room, where his father sat over the checkbook, and also into Mrs. Calloway's house. The old lady was still wearing her binoculars on the leather strap around her neck, although she couldn't see anything with them at night. She was feeding her goldfish. He didn't see why anybody'd pick goldfish over cats for pets; fish didn't *do* anything.

S.O.B. had disappeared, blending into the shadows. It wasn't completely dark, of course. There were the lights from the windows and a streetlight on the corner. Not that it would bother either Rob or the cat if it was dark.

Rob found a bunch of cherries and stripped them off the branch, eating them slowly, one by one. It was harder, in the dark, to see where the pits went, but he kept trying for Mrs. Calloway's window. One panel of the lace curtains had caught on something and was held to one side, so he could see in more clearly than usual. She'd finished feeding the fish and was putting a plate on the table for her solitary meal.

Rob watched, fascinated, as she lifted something that appeared to be a piece of raw liver to her mouth. He made a retching sound, and Mrs. Calloway looked up, directly at him.

She couldn't see him, of course; he was hidden by the leaves. Still, it made him feel funny to have her staring at him, when *he* could see *her* perfectly well.

She muttered something under her breath, apparently deciding what she'd heard was unimportant. Along with her raw liver, or whatever it was, she was having cauliflower. Rob twisted his face in disgust. Imagine eating liver and cauliflower if nobody made you do it.

As he watched, she dropped a section of the vegetable; it lodged in her binoculars, and when she'd removed it she took the glasses off over her head, too, and set them to one side. She must have forgotten she had them on. He thought she hung them around her neck first thing in the morning, the same time she put in her teeth.

A car stopped in front of the house. Without moving anything but his head, Rob watched as a man came up the sidewalk, hesitated, and then approached the lighted dining room windows.

It was his Uncle Ray, his mother's youngest brother. He was acting kind of funny, not going right in the way he usually did. Rob watched him, forgetting to blow out his cherry pit.

Uncle Ray reached up and scratched on the screen. "Walt! Hey, Walt!"

The hoarse whisper didn't seem to register for a moment. Then Mr. Mallory turned and frowned toward the window.

"Who's that?"

"It's me, Ray. Listen, I have to talk to you."

"Well, come on inside. What's all this scratching on the screen bit?"

"No, well, listen . . . Walt, it's important, and . . . and maybe it'd be better if Marge doesn't know I'm here. Maybe . . . maybe it'd be better if you came outside."

Mr. Mallory's frown deepened, but he stood up. "All right. I'll come out."

Rob could hear his mother's voice from the kitchen as his father passed through it, but couldn't make out the words. And then his father came down the back steps, caught S.O.B.'s tail on the bottom step, and nearly fell when the cat screeched and leaped for the cherry tree. There he found Rob and curled in his lap for some soothing pats, which Rob administered absent-mindedly.

"Darn cat . . . I said we ought to put him in a kennel over this weekend, anyway . . . maybe permanently. Like to broke my neck." Mr. Mallory peered through the gloom. "What's this all about?"

"Well . . ." Ray, who looked a lot like his sister, ran a hand through his dark hair in a nervous gesture. Rob blew a cherry pit at him, but it fell far short. "I . . . I've got a problem."

After a moment of waiting, Mr. Mallory prodded. "What kind of a problem?"

"Well . . . it's hard to talk about it, ac

Rob's father swore quietly. "Now listen, I've got plenty of things to do, so don't beat around the bush. What is it? Money? A girl? Don't tell me you've lost another job."

"Well . . . not yet."

This time the profanity was more explosive. "What do you mean, not yet? You're about to lose this job? For crying out loud, Ray, there's a limit to the number of jobs I can get you in this one small town! What have you done now?"

Ray's voice dropped so low that Rob, a few feet above him in the tree, could scarcely make out the words. "I . . . borrowed some money."

Rob couldn't see his father's face, but he knew what kind of expression went with that tone of voice. "You . . . borrowed some money. They don't fire you for . . . good grief, Ray, you didn't *steal money?* Tell me you didn't *steal* any money!"

Ray shifted his weight from one foot to the other. "It wasn't exactly . . . I was going to pay it back. I only needed it over the weekend. I thought sure I'd get it back, only . . . only it didn't work out. I tried to borrow against my car, but they said it wasn't worth that much . . ."

This time the curse carried a more ominous note. "How much? *How much money did you take?*"

"Twelve hundred dollars."

His father's echo was so soft that at first Rob thought he was unaffected by the amount, until he repeated it in a louder, outraged whisper. "Twelve hundred dollars? You swiped twelve hundred dollars? What for? No, never mind, don't tell me, I don't think

I want to know. And you can't raise that much on your car, and what do you want me to do about it? I'm marrying off a daughter day after tomorrow. Do you have any idea what that's done to my bank account? Champagne for 250 people? All the rest of it? Where do you think I'd come up with twelve hundred dollars on the spur of the moment?"

Rob listened to his father's raspy breathing and wished he'd let Uncle Ray tell what he used the money for. That ought to be interesting.

"It . . . isn't just the money. I mean, if I could pay it all back, I guess that would help . . . but French took the books and the cashbox home with him this weekend . . . by Monday he'll know the money's missing, and . . . and he'll know who had to have taken it . . ."

"You fool. You stupid fool," Mr. Mallory said.

"Don't you think I know that? Don't you think I've told myself . . ." Ray sounded as if he were about to cry.

"You're twenty-seven years old, and I swear you've got less sense than Robbie. He's constantly in trouble, but I'll have to admit a lot of it isn't his fault. But what excuse have you got? Twelve hundred dollars . . . I can't believe it!"

"I thought it was a sure thing I'd get it back, Walt. You don't understand . . ."

"No, and I don't want to, and that hardly matters anyway, does it? You can't put the money back because you don't have it, and even if you did, it's too late to do it without getting caught; so you're going to get fired . . . and probably prosecuted. That's what

25

it comes down to, isn't it? French will know you stole the money, and he'll call in the district attorney and ask for an indictment against you. And get it."

"Listen, French's a friend of yours," Ray said quickly, hopefully. "And you know Bill Sansome, too. You could talk to them, tell them I'll pay it back . . . what good would it do to put me in jail, make a mess in all the papers . . ."

"Why didn't you think of some of this before you took the money?"

"I told you, Walt, I thought I'd get the money back."

Mr. Mallory made a sound of disgust, deep in his throat, and turned away. Ray took a quick, nervous step after him.

"Listen, I know you haven't got that much cash, but Marge has those bonds Dad left her . . ."

Walt Mallory spun back, and now Rob could see his face. He'd never seen his father so angry. "No you don't. You don't touch Marge's bonds; and if you ask her for them, I'll break your neck. I mean it, Ray. And she's not to know anything about this, not until after the wedding, at least. She's got all she can handle right now, and I won't have Darcy's wedding spoiled. You hear me?"

Ray licked his lips. "Yeah, I hear you. But listen, Walt, you could call French, couldn't you? Maybe it wouldn't seem so bad if we contacted him before he actually discovers the shortage . . ."

Mr. Mallory spat. "Oh, sure. Tell him when he's on the verge of discovering it, when you know you can't conceal it any longer. That's a big inducement to forgive you, I'm sure. Ray, I never thought you were

26

overly bright, but even Robbie would have had better sense than this . . ."

Why *even Robbie*, as if an eleven year old was a retardo, or something? Rob frowned down at the pair.

"Listen, Walt, there's no telling what French will do when he finds it . . . he might call the police and have me picked up right then . . . this weekend . . . in the middle of the wedding, even!"

"Then maybe you'd better not come to the wedding. I haven't hit a man with my fist in years, Ray, but I sure will if your actions do anything to spoil the wedding for Darcy and Marge."

Rob had never thought of his father as hitting anyone with his fists. It was an interesting idea. Who had he hit, he wondered? And what for?

"Walt. Walt, I don't know anybody else to turn to, and I need help. Please, please, Walt . . . go talk to French. Before it's too late."

"You're a real man, aren't you? Not even 'come with me and talk to French,' just 'you go and talk to French.' Are you such a jelly-livered coward you aren't brave enough to go along and face the man yourself?"

"No, no, I didn't mean it that way . . . will you come? Will you talk to him . . . with me, of course?"

"If you weren't Marge's brother, I'd kick you all the way over there. I ought to do it, anyway," Mr. Mallory said, but he was giving in. "I'll have to tell Marge I'm going out for a while. You stay out here."

In a few minutes they were gone and all was quiet. Even Mrs. Calloway had turned off her dining room light, although she was moving around in the kitchen, out of Rob's sight. After a time S.O.B. decided he had been petted enough to make up for his wounded tail and feelings and he took off on one of his nightly escapades.

Fifteen minutes after Uncle Ray's car drove off, Steve's eased into the same parking space. Rob sighed. He'd be glad when the wedding was over and all the people went somewhere else. Steve and Darcy off on their honeymoon and then to their own apartment. And once Darcy was gone, old Max and Derek would quit coming around, too. Then maybe there'd be some peace and quiet and meals on time.

Speaking of meals, he was beginning to get hungry again. He wondered if anybody'd got any more bread so he could make a sandwich. He was about to slide out of the tree when Steve and Darcy came up along the side of the house. It was a shame they hadn't put the sidewalk on the other side, away from the cherry tree.

"It's too nice a night to go in," Darcy said, sounding dreamy, the way she did most of the time these days, except when she was screaming in a panic about something. "Let's sit here on the bench for a while."

"Suits me. Almost anything you'd say suits me," Steve told her.

Rob had the choice of dropping on top of them or staying where he was. He hoped they weren't going to get too mushy. He'd throw up all over them. It was an entertaining idea, he decided.

Their words were low, intended only for one another, but they carried to Rob in the tree above them. He couldn't stand very much of it, and he picked an entire handful of cherries and dropped them, all at once, in a shower over the couple.

That ended the silly exchange of words. They looked up, laughing, although they couldn't see him in the dimness of the branches.

"Okay chum, we get the message," Steve said. "We'll move along and leave you in peace." They moved off, and Rob decided he might move, too.

He made to descend and caught a glimpse of S.O.B. streaking across the yard toward Mrs. Calloway's. Cripes. He supposed he'd better go get him; if he got into any more trouble they might really put him in a kennel for the weekend, and that would about kill old S.O.B.

His sneakers hit the ground with barely a thud. He rounded the corner of the house next door, pausing to look around. It wasn't so light back here, but he could make out the big dark blob of fur . . . right on the old lady's doorstep, for cripes sake. Wouldn't that dumb cat ever learn?

When he got right next to the back porch, though, he saw what had drawn the animal. His resentment against Mrs. Calloway rose to a peak of indignation. She put bones and meat scraps in her garbage can, and when it was too full she just left the lid off. It was like she was setting a trap for a cat, for crying out loud, to leave meat scraps in the open like that.

"S.O.B.! Come 'ere!"

The cat had dragged something out of the garbage and was chewing on it with evident relish, paying no attention to Rob. He put one foot on the bottom step, reaching up for the cat.

It was at that point that all hell broke loose.

3

He didn't know where she'd been hiding, but there was no doubt the old witch had been waiting for them . . . Rob and the cat. She pounced with a triumphant cry, and the broom crashed down on Rob's head. It scratched the side of his face, and then was lifted and brought down again and again, slashing at him, pounding, jabbing, and all the while she was yelling and screaming at him.

S.O.B. gave one startled yowl and vanished; it was a little longer before Rob, falling backward down the steps, could get out of the woman's reach. She stood panting above him as he sprawled on the cement with something sharp poking into his flank.

"That'll teach you to stay off my property, you nasty little wretch! You and your confounded dirty cat!"

She spat at him, and the spittle struck him on the cheek, and then she brought the upended broom down one more time; he rolled aside, or she might have stuck it right through him.

Rob struggled for breath, unable to answer before

she had taken her broom and gone back into the house.

He hurt all over, and something was trickling into his eyes. *Cripes, she might have killed me*, he thought, and managed to turn over and get to his feet.

He created quite a sensation when he walked into the house. For once they noticed him.

His mother sprang to her feet with a cry. "Rob! For heaven's sake, what's happened to you?"

They were all there; his father had come home, and Teddi and old Max, and Darcy and Steve, and even Derek was still there, all milling around.

"Rob . . . what happened, son?" Walt Mallory swept the others aside as if they were a swarm of gnats, tipping Rob's chin so that he could see the damage.

He told them while his mother ran for a washcloth and got the blood out of his eyes.

"Why, that old witch! Wally, call the police! She might have put his eye out!"

Darcy was staring at him in dismay. "Good grief, how's he going to look in the wedding pictures? Mom, he's getting a *black eye*!"

"That's better than losing one," her father pointed out. "Teddi, get some gauze and some tape."

"Don't you think we'd better get him to a doctor, Wally? It's a nasty gash . . . maybe it should be stitched."

"No, I don't think the damage is that serious. We can pull it together with tape, I think. Wouldn't you say so, Steve?"

Steve was an expert because he'd been a medic in

the Marines. He looked the cut over soberly, nodding. "Yes, sir, I think so. It's not deep. Head cuts usually bleed pretty bad, but I don't think he needs stitches."

Mr. Mallory plastered the washcloth against the wound. "There, hold it there, son. You want to sit down?"

He was feeling sort of wobbly. "Yeah, I guess."

"Aren't you going to call the police?"

His father sighed. "No, I don't think so, Marge. After all, Rob was on her property. And he's been told to stay off it."

"But he only went over to bring back the cat . . . and from what he says, she'd deliberately enticed S.O.B. over there." His mother really looked mad. He was glad to see she still cared. He'd begun to wonder a little. "Wally, we aren't just going to let her get away with it, are we?"

"Do you really want to take on a major battle right now? This weekend? It will mean having a doctor check Rob over . . . although he's not seriously hurt . . . and having police all over the place, probably for hours. And eventually we'd have to go to court, testify against her . . ."

"Somebody ought to testify against her," Max said sourly. "Boy, that woman's crazy!"

"She's a witch," Rob said. "She eats raw liver . . . I saw her. The blood ran down her chin." It seemed to him that it really had. "She's a real witch."

"Robbie!" Teddi protested. "She couldn't have eaten raw liver!"

"She did, tonight. I saw her. Is my eye really getting black?" It would be rather nice if it was.

32

Darcy moaned. "He's going to look terrible . . . he'll ruin my wedding pictures!"

"Oh, for heaven's sake, Darcy!" Mrs. Mallory scowled. "Naturally you want nice pictures, but he didn't do it on purpose, you know!"

"As a matter of fact," Steve said, "I think Rob will add a good deal of interest to what will probably be a very dull afternoon. He'll be a conversation piece."

"A dull afternoon!" Darcy cried. "Well, if that's the way you feel about it! . . ."

Steve smiled at her. "Darling, shut up. You hear me? Shut up."

Shocked, for once she kept quiet.

"What's a conversation piece?" Rob asked.

"It's something people talk about," Steve told him. "What happened to S.O.B., Rob? Did he get clobbered, too?"

"I heard him yowl the first time she swung the broom. I guess he got away after that. I think he did. Should I go look for his body?"

"Not if it involves going back onto Mrs. Calloway's property," his mother said quickly. "Better a dead cat than a dead boy."

"I'm sure S.O.B.'s quite all right," Walt Mallory said wearily. "Look, Rob's okay. Go call the cat, if you want to, and make sure he's okay, too. But let's not start a ruckus right now with Mrs. Calloway. Not before the wedding. We've already got enough problems to handle."

Mrs. Mallory looked at Rob uncertainly. "Are we just going to let her get away with it, then?"

"No. But we'll wait until we've got time to breathe.

The old woman's getting dangerous, if she'll entice the cat and then attack it and anyone who comes after it. Maybe she ought to be certified, I don't know. I'll talk to Bill Sansome sometime next week, ask him what we ought to do. But not now, okay?"

"I think I'd better see if S.O.B.'s still out there," Rob said. He moved slyly to where he could see his own reflection in the mirror over the buffet. There was a nice big mark around his left eye, although it didn't really hurt much any more, and the assorted cuts and scratches would be impressive when he told the story to his friends. She was a real witch, eating raw liver and trying to spear him or beat him to death with the broom. "I want to make sure he's okay."

"Wally . . ."

"It's all right. I'll go with him. Come on, let's find the big son-of-a-gun. I wish we had someplace to lock him up for a few days."

"It wasn't his fault, Dad. She put meat scraps and stuff out where he'd smell it."

"Yeah, well, let's get him inside and away from her for a while." They went out into the yard together, squinting to see a darker mass among the shadows. "Call him, Rob. He's more likely to come for you."

S.O.B. was there, in the cherry tree. Rob reached up and brought him down, cradling him as if he were a baby. "Mean old witch, did she scare you half to death? Dad?"

"Yes?" His father paused at the foot of the back steps.

"Is Uncle Ray going to jail?"

His father flinched slightly. "So you heard that, did

you? Where were you? Up the tree?"

"Is he? Are they going to put him in jail?"

"I don't know what they're going to do to him. Nobody knows yet that he took the money. We tried to see French, but he wasn't home."

"Will you be able to talk him out of putting Uncle Ray in jail, do you think? He's a friend of yours."

"Yes. He's a friend. And for that reason I don't know if I have a right to ask him not to prosecute. He's got a right to do that. A right to be pretty mad, too. As far as Ray goes, it would probably do him good to see what happens to people who steal. On the other hand, it would hurt your mother very much if he went to jail. So I don't know what will happen."

"Would they put him in jail for very long, for stealing twelve hundred dollars?"

"I don't know, Rob. Listen, this is just between us, understand? Not a word to anyone else, not until after the wedding. And then I'll tell your mother. You keep your mouth shut."

"Sure. I understand."

"Okay. Why don't you go on up and take your bath and go to bed, now."

"But it's only 9:30!"

"That's late enough, considering we've all got to be up early and get a lot of things done. Please, Rob. If you don't feel like sleeping, watch TV or read something. But get out of everybody's sight for a while, let 'em cool off, will you?"

He felt sort of resentful about that. *Let them cool off*, as if he'd done something terrible. It wasn't *him*, it was Mrs. Calloway, or even S.O.B. They'd have been madder yet if he'd just let the cat go over there and not tried to stop him, he thought, climbing the stairs.

His window was over the porch. He could hear Teddi down there with old Max, giggling. Cripes. Now that Darcy was almost gone, was it going to start all over again with Teddi?

He began to undress in front of his own mirror, leaning close to check, once more, the injuries inflicted on him by that witch next door.

"She could have killed me," he said to his image, scowling. "For all she knows, she did. She didn't even wait to see if I was able to get up."

He stood there, his shirt halfway off; it seemed to him that, as he watched, the bruise around his eye deepened in color. Cripes, she could have put his eye out, blinded him for life. He pulled up his T-shirt and inspected his flank, where he'd taken a solid jab from the broom handle. That was turning purple, too. It's a wonder she didn't break his ribs. For such a little woman, she sure packed a wallop.

It would have served her right if she'd killed him and they'd put her in jail for life. Only probably she'd have pleaded not guilty by reason of insanity. He guessed anybody would believe that, that she was insane. Only a nut would eat raw liver and let the blood run off her chin and attack people with a broom.

He wondered if you could get off on a charge of stealing by pleading not guilty by reason of insanity. He supposed not, or his father would have thought of it.

Would they still have had the wedding if she'd

killed him? Boy, that would really have ticked Darcy off, if they'd had to call off the wedding.

A little blood was seeping through the bandage they'd put on his forehead. Cripes, if she'd knocked him out, he might have laid there until he bled to death. For all she knew, he was still out there at the foot of her steps, bleeding his life away.

He stared at his reflection, and gradually a grin began to spread over his face. He'd fix her. By golly, he'd fix her. Maybe he'd even scare her into having a fit.

4

It wasn't difficult to arrange, really. He knew they used catsup for blood, in the movies. He'd seen a show about how they did it. There was plenty of catsup in the kitchen. That was about all the props he needed.

The time to do it was right at seven o'clock in the morning. The paper boy delivered her *Chronicle* between 6:50 and 6:55 every day. Most people got their papers on their front porches or lawns, but Mrs. Calloway didn't because she said the neighbors stole it when it was left out front. Her paper boy was Matt Papovich, and he'd just as soon not have delivered any paper to her at all, because she complained no matter what he did and he always had to come back three times to get paid. Three times, every month. She insisted that he put the paper on her back porch, and he couldn't throw it from the alley, either, because then he knocked down her chrysanthemums or something. He had to walk right up and put the paper on the porch.

At exactly seven o'clock, Mrs. Calloway would come

out for her paper. And today, Rob thought with a sense of delight, she would find a dead boy on her steps . . . a murdered boy. He wondered if he'd dare keep his eyes partway open so he could see the look on her face when she found him. He hoped he scared her bad enough so she'd have a fit.

He almost forgot to take the bandage off his head. That would really do it, he thought disgustedly, wincing as the tape came off. It was disappointing-looking this morning, not nearly as nasty as it had looked last night. He wished the kids could have seen it last night.

He couldn't very well put the catsup on until he was lying down, or it would run in all the wrong places. And he should be sure the paper was there ahead of time, so that Matt wouldn't find him first. He didn't want anybody to see him except Mrs. Calloway.

He hoped Matt wouldn't be late with the paper.

The house was quiet as he made his way down the stairs. It was going to be hot today; it was already warm, at a quarter of seven. He considered taking time to fix something to eat, then decided it would take too long. This was a split-second operation, and it had to be done this morning. After today, it wouldn't work. Not as well, anyway; she wouldn't think she'd done it herself unless he was there when she came out this morning.

He let himself out onto the porch, catsup bottle in one hand, and waited, watching the back alley. And there came Matt . . . not late, but a few minutes early. He walked up and put the paper on the back porch. Then, as an afterthought, he picked it up again, spit on it, and put it back.

Rob waited until he'd gone, then eased open the screen door. The grass wasn't even damp, the air was so dry. He heard S.O.B.'s cry and looked up to see the cat on the edge of the roof, looking ready to jump off into the cherry tree.

"Shut up, stupid, you'll wake somebody up," Rob told him softly, and continued across the yard to the back of the Calloway house.

He'd intended to be found sprawled on the steps, because it seemed more dramatic that way, but he found that it was horribly uncomfortable. A guy could cripple himself forever, lying on his back on the steps for very long.

It would have to be on the sidewalk at the bottom, then. Maybe he could just have his legs up on the steps. Rob squirmed around, trying out several positions, wishing he could think of some way to do it so it would look like his legs were broken. He couldn't, not without really hurting them.

Finally he thought he had it. He took the top off the catsup bottle and liberally laced his face with it. Then, for good measure, he poured some on his shirt-front, too. He'd worn a white shirt, so it would show up better. The old woman had attacked him in the dark; she wouldn't know what he was wearing last night.

As a final step, he threw the catsup bottle as far as he could. He'd forgotten to put the cap back on and its contents spewed across the grass, but maybe she wouldn't notice that. She'd be too busy seeing the body in front of her.

He didn't have a watch to check the time, but it must be pretty close to seven. He hoped she'd come out pretty soon; it was hard to lie still, and the catsup was running sort of close to one eye. He didn't know if he could wipe it without messing up the whole effect.

Something touched him on one ear and he almost yelped aloud before he recognized S.O.B.

"For pete's sake, you dumb cat, get out of here!"

S.O.B. surveyed him with great unblinking yellow eyes only inches from his own. Rob pushed at him with one outthrust hand. "Beat it! Go on! Scat!"

And then he heard her coming, heard her shuffling footsteps beyond the door, and he froze, trying to look pale beneath his bloody wounds.

He couldn't resist opening one eye just a little, to see how she reacted. Maybe she'd have a heart attack, and fall right down on top of him . . .

The door swung inward, and Mrs. Calloway stepped out onto the porch. She was wearing a ratty-looking bathrobe and slippers that must have belonged to her husband before he died. They almost fell off her feet when she moved. She stooped to pick up her paper, and then she saw him.

For a few seconds she was poised in mid-stride, as if she were in a movie someone had brought to a stop. The only thing that moved was her jaw, which dropped.

And then, before she could have a fit or a heart attack or anything interesting, someone began to scream from his own house next door.

He'd counted on scaring Mrs. Calloway and getting back home before anybody else got up. How could he have guessed that Darcy wouldn't be able to sleep, that she'd get up and look out her window and see him?

Nobody was dressed. They all came pouring out of the house in their nightclothes, with Darcy reaching him first because she'd been the one to spot him. She was wearing a short nightgown of pale blue nylon. She stopped a few feet away, her eyes wide, chest heaving, and gradually her horror was replaced by an expression of fury so intense Rob thought she was going to throttle him then and there.

Probably she would have, if their parents hadn't arrived right behind her.

"It's catsup!" Darcy shrieked. "You rotten little beast, I thought you were dead!"

Across the alley Mr. Wentworth called out sleepily, "What's going on out there?" Nobody answered him.

Rob sat up. It was all spoiled, everyone running out like that, Darcy yelling her fool head off. As he sat up, the catsup began to run and he didn't have anything to wipe it with except his hands, so it got pretty messy.

"Rob, what's got into you!" His father jerked him to his feet, propelling him toward the house. "Get back inside! All of you, and Darcy, stop that racket before I smack you!"

Rob twisted his head, trying to see what Mrs. Calloway was doing, but his father wasn't allowing him any time for that. The hand that grabbed his arm was strong enough to tear the arm off, and for a moment he thought that was what might happen.

His mother had only come as far as the back steps; she stood holding the door open, and they were all hustled inside, beyond the view of the neighbors who were beginning to filter out of their houses.

Walt Mallory's face was white. "Confound you, Rob, I ought to beat the tar out of you!"

"I thought he was dead!" Darcy exploded, letting the screen slam behind her. "What a rotten thing to do! Scaring us all half to death!"

"Your screaming was a big help," her father informed her, pushing them all ahead of him into the kitchen. "Rob, get that mess washed off yourself, and then we'd better have a little talk."

"What were you doing?" Teddi demanded. "Boy, you really look awful. No wonder Darcy screamed."

He was allowed to go into the bathroom and wash; he stripped off his shirt and his T-shirt, because there wasn't much he could do about them. Cripes. He might have known something would go wrong. He didn't even know how Mrs. Calloway had reacted.

They were all there in the kitchen when he came out, still standing around waiting for him. His mother was making coffee. His father looked very tired, as if he hadn't slept well.

"You want to tell us, now, what you thought you were doing?"

Rob tried to explain. It seemed perfectly reasonable to him, but he didn't see any signs of understanding on any of their faces. Only Teddi showed some sympathy, but even most of that seemed to be for Darcy, who had "discovered" him.

"Rob, can't you get it through your head? We don't want any more trouble with Mrs. Calloway. We've got problems enough already. We want you to stay strictly away from her. Is that clear? Stay off her property, don't look in her windows, don't speak to her, *stay out of her sight!*"

43

Rob stood perfectly still. He hadn't made up his mind yet what to say. He thought they were being completely unfair. Cripes, nobody did anything when she attacked him, but when he tried to get even a little, wham! Everything hit the fan.

The telephone chime drew Darcy in a swirl of blue nylon. Rob still hadn't thought up any reply to his father that wouldn't be mad or resentful, and from the looks around him it didn't seem the time to be either. And then he didn't have to say anything, because the telephone call took all the attention.

Darcy cried, "Oh, *no!*" her voice climbing as if she were in pain.

"Now what?" Mrs. Mallory demanded. "Go on, all of you, get dressed."

"I wasn't planning to get up this early," Teddi protested.

"Well, you're up now, so get dressed and let's get this show on the road," her father ordered. "You've got a list of stuff we still have to do today?" he asked turning to Mrs. Mallory.

"A mile long," she answered, her mouth forming a flat line.

From the dining room Darcy's voice rose in an anguished wail. "What am I going to *do?*"

Her father paused in the doorway on his way upstairs to dress. "For starters, you might stop waking up all the neighbors. And get some clothes on."

It was as if she hadn't heard him. Her blue eyes were wide and filling with tears. "Daddy, Nancy's got the measles! *Measles!*"

"Well, I'm sorry, but she's only one of the brides-

44

maids, isn't she? You've still got three other ones."

"You don't understand! We've got four ushers, too, and there have to be the same number! The *measles*!" Her face crumpled as her father took the phone out of her hand and put it down.

"The rehearsal isn't until 7:30 tonight," Mrs. Mallory said briskly, assuming control. "You'll just have to find someone to take her place."

"But where will I find anybody who can wear her *dress*? Mother, you know how skinny she is! There's nobody else in town who'll fit into that dress!"

"How about Ellen Anderson?" Teddi suggested. Rob began to ease backward toward the door, hoping he could escape to the hall before anybody noticed he was going.

"Oh, Teddi, you know I haven't spoken to her since that fight last fall!"

"Maybe now would be a good time to start speaking again, if she's the only one in town who can wear the dress," Mr. Mallory suggested.

Rob made it to the hall door, then sped up the stairs, leaving them discussing the problem. He stood at his window, looking out over the side lawn, hating the old woman next door. It wasn't fair that she should be able to attack him that way and then they should all be mad at *him* for trying to get just a little bit even.

He put on a clean shirt, absently licking off a bit of catsup he'd missed on his forearm. He'd be better off staying up here, but he was hungry. Maybe they were all in such a mess down there, with the new crisis, that they would forget about him.

S.O.B. came through the window from the roof, landing on the bed without a sound. Rob glowered at him.

"It's all your fault. If you weren't so stupid, and didn't get into her garbage can . . ."

The cat began to wash himself, uncaring, and Rob sighed. "I guess it's really *her* fault . . . but nobody will do anything about *her*."

By the time he got back down to the kitchen, the wedding crises had multiplied. There was a telegram from Aunt Sylvia, which Teddi read aloud in dramatic accents.

"Sylvester doesn't have to work after all, so we're *all* coming."

Mrs. Mallory paused in the midst of pouring pancake batter onto the griddle. "*All* of them? All *seven* of them? But I was only expecting Sylvia . . . good grief, where am I going to come up with beds for an extra six people on such short notice?"

Her husband had dressed and was helping out by setting the table. "Get out all the sleeping bags. Put the kids on the floors."

"But that still leaves Sylvester left over . . . you know how he'd react to being put on the floor!"

"Put him in Rob's room, with Nick, then. Let Rob sleep on the floor."

Rob winced from the eyes that flicked in his direction, but at least nobody looked as if they were going to hit him right that minute.

"I guess I could do that. Here, who's ready to start?"

"Can I have the first ones?" Rob asked quickly. Again he got that raking over by hostile glances, but his mother handed him the plate. He considered, decided the atmosphere needed cooling, and that it would be better to eat outside. He slathered butter on the hotcakes, laced them liberally with brown sugar, and rolled them up so they could be eaten in his hand. His mother opened her mouth to protest when she saw him heading for the door, but luckily the phone rang again.

"Listen, somebody has to be at the church to let in the florist," Darcy was saying.

"Can't they get in during rehearsal?"

"No, they said around 5:00. They want to set up the baskets and stuff then. They only have one man working tomorrow, and all he'll do is put the flowers in the baskets. I can't be there, Mother, I've got to see what I can do about a bridesmaid, and Steve said . . ."

Rob let the door slam behind him. Boy, he'd sure be glad when this weekend was over.

He munched through the pancakes, wishing he had two more. Was it worth it to go back inside for seconds? Maybe it would be better to wait a little while, till they'd cleared out.

Mrs. Calloway stood on her back steps, holding her binoculars to her eyes. The old bag, he thought, and kicked at the hose that lay across the sidewalk.

"Rob . . . hook up the sprinkler there on the front lawn, will you?"

He grunted and made his way toward the street, alternately kicking the hose and the sprinkler ahead of him. When he got in under the shrubbery to turn on the water, a big spider got on his hand and he brushed it off. Too bad he couldn't take all his spiders and put them in Mrs. Calloway's house. He bet she'd have a fit over that, all right, if they were running all over her bed. He imagined them, dumped on her while she was sleeping, seeing them run into her ears and up her nose and into her mouth, which would be open while she was snoring. He knew she snored, he'd heard her. It made him feel better to think of her with spiders in her mouth, and he turned on the water and was starting back around the house when his father bellowed from the front porch.

"Rob! Not right on the sidewalk! Not when we've got people coming and going all day!"

Knowing there was no point in saying anything, Rob turned back and moved the sprinkler. He hardly had it on the sidewalk at all. If anybody hurried, they wouldn't get more than slightly damp. Hot as it was, you wouldn't think that would bother anybody, but there was no explaining grown-ups.

A car door slammed and he looked over his shoulder to see his Aunt Grace coming up the walk. Yes, he'd sure be glad when this was all over. People coming and going every minute, and every time he turned around they wanted him to do something.

"Hello, Grace. What are you doing up so early?"

"Walt, do you know what's going on?"

His father sounded wary. "In regard to what, Grace?"

"In regard to Ray. He's gone and run off or something . . . is he in trouble of some kind?"

Rob paused to listen, just around the corner of the house.

48

"Run off? What makes you think he's run off?"

"His car's gone, and he took a suitcase and most of his good clothes. He didn't leave a note or anything, but . . . well, Ma's having a fit because he won't be at the wedding. I'm more concerned about why he left in the first place. Is he running away from somebody?"

"Oh no! That stupid idiot . . ."

"He is in trouble, then. What did he do?"

"He 'borrowed' some money from his boss, that's what he did, and he knows French is going to discover the loss this weekend . . . You got any idea where he went?"

The water was sprinkling on Rob, but he didn't care. The water wasn't very cold. He stayed where he was, listening.

"Maybe over to that girl's he's been going with. I don't know where else. Walt, he's going to be in worse trouble if he runs away, isn't he? Maybe somebody ought to go after him."

"Grace, do you have any idea how many things Marge has lined up for me to do today? I have to get the champagne and ice it down, be at both the reception hall and the church to let in the florist, round up a set of candelabra from St. Thomas's and bring them over to our church . . . oh, the heck with it! Who is this girl? Where does she live?"

Rob shrugged, going on around the house.

From the back porch Teddi was calling. "Rob! Robbie, where are you? Mother wants you to get your room cleaned up! You'll have to change both beds!"

By the time that was done he had made up his

mind. He wasn't staying around to fetch and carry for this bunch of females. He stuffed his pockets with cookies, made two bologna sandwiches with mustard and Swiss cheese, and as an afterthought fished a Pepsi out of the refrigerator.

It wasn't easy to get up there with his hands so full, but he made it. He'd spend the rest of the day in the cherry tree, until it was time for all of them to go to the rehearsal. Then he'd climb down and get something more to eat.

There was a broad, almost flat place on one limb, right close to the trunk. He could put the Pepsi down there after he'd pried the cap off. He kept a bottle opener hanging up there on a string for just such emergencies. A guy never knew when he might need to open a bottle.

He spent the next hour in the cherry tree.

That was how he happened to see the murder.

5

He was getting better at spitting cherry pits. He got a few of them onto Mrs. Calloway's windowsill. Of course he cheated, moving a little further along the big branch than usual. But it was worth it.

S.O.B. yowled at him, eyeing the sandwich. Rob broke off a corner and extended it, then put it down on a branch where the cat could pick it up by himself. S.O.B. expertly sought out the meat, then shook his head, flattening his ears, moving away. He stared with contemptuous yellow eyes, tail twitching his displeasure.

"I like it with mustard," Rob informed him. "If you're so fussy, make your own sandwiches."

Somewhere in Mrs. Calloway's house someone turned on the phonograph. It was an old, tinny-sounding thing, and she must be deaf because it was turned up sort of loud. He remembered one time when Teddi had been playing her stereo that loud and the old witch called the police.

He thought about calling the police on *her*, but he

knew at once they wouldn't like that, either. They'd be mad at him no matter what he did.

"I will not," Mrs. Calloway said sharply.

Rob shifted position a little, so that he could rest his back against the tree trunk. The lace curtains weren't blowing much today, and he couldn't see into her house except when she came right close to the window.

She did this now, pushing aside the limp lace to stare down at the cherry pits.

"Such a nasty little boy. I can't think why they tolerate him," she said, her mouth curling with distaste. The binoculars swung on their strap against her scrawny bosom. "How does he get them up here on my windowsill?"

He thought he heard someone say something to her, but it was hard to tell, with the music playing, all loud and scratchy the way it was.

She turned her head, and this time he was sure there was someone in the room with her, for she said, "You must be out of your mind to think I'd agree to any such thing."

She had reached to one side and scooped up a newspaper from the table; now she used it to push the cherry pits off onto the ground, her lips clamped tightly together.

S.O.B. saw the movement and began to creep toward her, out along the big limb. Rob opened his mouth to speak, to call him back, but already it was too late. The old woman had spotted the cat, and Rob hated to give away his own position. If she knew he spent so much time up the tree, she'd have him arrested for being a Peeping Tom or something, and then they wouldn't let him sit here anymore.

"Go on! Get away, you nasty thing!"

She leaned toward him, her head and shoulders out the window, swatting at the cat. S.O.B. was a hardened customer, however; unafraid, he was poised to spring.

Rob slid one foot downward, seeking the limb he knew was there, ready to reach out and grab the cat, when it happened.

It was so fast he could hardly take in what he had seen, although later he was able to put it all together as if in slow motion. It took much longer to tell about it than it did to happen.

Mrs. Calloway was leaning through the window, with S.O.B. ready to spring. (Perhaps he remembered the taste of that goldfish, and that there were more of them in there, through that open window.) Suddenly the old lady was lifted off her feet, through the opening, surprise causing her to emit a small squeak. That's all, only a squeak, like a cornered mouse.

For just a second Rob saw the hands that had pushed her . . . big hands, a man's hands, surely . . . and S.O.B., alarmed by the figure coming toward him, bounded from the branch into the house. Rob heard a muffled grunt, saw the cat disappear and blood oozing up in ridges on the man's forearms where S.O.B.'s claws had raked him. And then the arms were gone, the lace curtain hung limply across the opening, and he couldn't see into the house any longer.

All of that he saw, in seconds . . . less than seconds . . . while Mrs. Calloway was falling, flailing with her arms and legs, and then she gave a gurgling, choked cry and was silent.

Rob stared down into her face, which was looking straight up at him and slowly turning blue. The leather strap of the binoculars had twisted about her neck, and as she fell had caught around the big branch, the one that had been cut off when it approached the side of her house; it was thick, thick enough to hold her meager weight as she swung there, her toes dangling only a foot or two off the ground.

Her glasses had gone askew, tipped by a branch or perhaps one of her own clawing hands, for she tried to loosen the strap at her neck. Her eyes, up close, were a pale blue; they bulged as if they were being squeezed out of her, and her mouth gaped, working soundlessly, then not at all.

Rob was frozen above her in the tree, looking down, unbelieving as the intelligence in the eyes, the fear, the agony, faded. He opened his mouth, trying to yell because he could hear people behind him at his own house, but he couldn't make any noise. Not even a squeak.

The bulging eyes continued to stare up at him, sightless now. He knew they couldn't see him. The small body swung gently, turning a little, on the leather strap.

His chest hurt, as if his own breathing had been cut off. Rob shot one frantic glance after S.O.B., but there was no way of getting him back, short of climbing over that awful swinging body, which he could not do. If they found the cat in the house maybe they'd say it was his fault, and they'd put him to sleep or something . . . He ought to go after the cat, and he couldn't. He couldn't speak, he couldn't move.

And then his foot slipped, and he fell forward, almost onto . . . it. Already he thought of her that way . . . as *it*. Not a person, but a thing. He actually brushed against the swinging body as he fell. He didn't feel the twigs that scraped his face and his arms, didn't know when he struck the ground. He doubled his legs under him, and they took him toward the back door; his hands didn't seem to work right as he scrabbled with the door, and he stumbled going across the threshold.

The house was full of people, their faces blurring before his eyes.

"Leave the pieces, huh, boy?" Mr. Mallory bent over to right a chair Rob didn't even know he'd overturned. "Where have you been? Your mother wanted you to . . ."

It didn't register, whatever his mother wanted him to do. It took two tries before the words came, gasping, puffing, almost not words at all.

"She's dead! Mrs. Calloway is dead! She's hanging in the cherry tree!"

None of their faces changed. Mr. Mallory sighed, shaking his head slightly. "Rob, I'm sorry if this weekend is boring you, but the rest of us are busy and we haven't got time for any more of your foolishness, do you understand?"

There seemed to be a roaring noise in his ears, as if something were gushing through his head, under pressure.

"No, it's not . . . I'm . . . Dad, she really is dead! She's hanging in the cherry tree! And S.O.B. went through her window, he's in her house . . . he didn't have anything to do with it, honest he didn't . . . but she's just . . . hanging there . . . and her eyes are squeezed out!"

They really looked at him, then.

Mrs. Mallory rose slowly from the chair where she had been sitting, hemming Darcy's dress. "Robert Walter Mallory, if you're making this up . . ."

He shook his head, pleading for them to believe him, feeling as if he'd been running for blocks. "I'm not, Mom! She's dead, she's really dead!"

The color left his mother's face. "Maybe you'd better go see, Wally."

Their faces reflected, now, his own horror. They were beginning to believe, at least that he *thought* what he was saying was the truth.

"How could you possibly know . . ." Darcy asked slowly.

"I know. I was . . . looking at her, when she died."

His words echoed hollowly. Mr. Mallory moved toward the door, not running but moving fast, and the rest of them followed. Rob didn't know if he wanted to go out there again or not. He had a horrid notion that he was going to dream about Mrs. Calloway, swinging and swaying from the branch of the cherry tree, with her eyes bugging out. He felt a little sick to his stomach.

They poured out into the sunlit yard like a swarm of ants over spilled syrup, and then slowed. His father had reached her, put his arms up, lifting the frail old body. Funny, how little she looked. Rob had never thought of her as being so tiny.

Walt Mallory looked toward the house. "Come here, somebody . . . Steve, give me a hand, get that damned strap off of there . . . Teddi, call the ambulance."

Teddi was halfway back to the house when he followed that up with a final command. "Better call the police, too, I guess."

With Steve freeing the strap from the stump of the limb, the old woman was lifted down and stretched out on the grass. Rob stayed where he was, beside his own house. He could see all he wanted to see from there. He wondered if S.O.B. would come if they called him at the open window, but he didn't want to walk over so close to . . . it . . . to find out.

Mr. Mallory and Steve were kneeling beside the old woman. His mother, who had gone halfway to them, called out, "Is she . . . is she really? . . ."

Mr. Mallory stood up. "Yes, looks like she strangled on that confounded binocular strap. Of all the stupid things . . . there isn't anything anybody can do for her now, I'm afraid."

Mrs. Mallory retreated to Rob's side, putting one hand on his shoulder. She was trembling.

"Dear heaven . . . of all the times for such a thing to happen . . . what *did* happen, Rob? She just fell out the window?"

He opened his mouth, but Teddi's words covered his own as she came running back outside. "They're coming, both of them, the ambulance and the police! Is she really dead?"

Steve came toward them across the grass. "She's

dead, all right. Man, talk about a freaky accident . . . another foot and she'd have been able to stand up."

"Hey, what's going on? Holding a convention?"

They all looked toward the street, where Max was coming toward them, smiling. "I had such a hassle with Old Lady Calloway yesterday, I thought I'd better park around the corner this time. What's going on?"

He read their expressions, then, and a moment later spotted the limp small figure on the grass. "Hey, what happened?"

"It's Mrs. Calloway," Teddi said, torn between horror and excitement. "I called an ambulance, but Daddy and Steve say she's dead."

Max swallowed. "How come? I mean, what happened?"

"She fell out the window and hanged herself in the cherry tree with the binocular straps," Steve explained. "Rob saw her fall. I wouldn't go look at her if I were you; she isn't pretty."

"I have no desire to look at her," Max assured him. "Holy moley, what a thing to happen."

Behind them, in the house, the telephone began to chime. For a moment nobody moved.

"Teddi, get the phone." His mother might have been rooted there beside him, her fingers digging into his shoulder. "Dear God, I don't think I can take much more today. There are the sirens. Now I suppose everybody within blocks will be out here."

Mr. Mallory was still standing beside the body. "Yes. Why don't you all go in the house? I'll talk to them when they come."

"Darcy!" Teddi poked her head out a window. "It's the bakery calling back. There's been some kind of mix-up on your cake; they had the date down wrong, for *next* Saturday."

Darcy, who was already pale, began to shake. "They couldn't have it wrong. They couldn't! I saw them mark it in the book, the seventeenth, I *saw* it!"

"Well, I don't know, that's what they said! Somebody better talk to them!"

Mrs. Mallory inhaled deeply, releasing Rob. "Well, if they made a mistake they'd better start working double-time, because they're going to have a cake to feed three hundred people at the reception hall by noon tomorrow, or else!"

"Will you talk to them, Darcy?"

"Mom . . . please, Mom . . ." Darcy looked as if she were going to cry.

"Don't worry, they'll have a cake if they all have to stay up all night making it." Mrs. Mallory strode up the steps, in a way that made Rob glad it wasn't him she was mad at.

Rob stood where he was as the rest of the family reentered the house, listening to the approaching sirens. They were almost here, and he hadn't gotten S.O.B. out of the house next door, and maybe they'd seal it up or something, and the cat wouldn't be able to get out . . .

And then he saw him. S.O.B., creeping along the side of Mrs. Calloway's house. Rob felt a slight relaxation of his muscles. At least the cat had come out; he wouldn't be trapped in there.

He watched his father meet the police at the curb.

There were two of them, both men his father knew. They talked for a minute, there on the sidewalk, and then they all walked up to stand over Mrs. Calloway. One of them was shaking his head.

It was about then that Rob began to go over the events in his mind. How Old Lady Calloway had been leaning out the window and those hands had come out and pushed her, and old S.O.B. had scratched the man on the arms.

He understood how anybody might have wanted to push her out the window. And it wasn't as if anybody could expect to *murder* her that way. As Steve had remarked, she might not have been hurt at all if she'd fallen to the ground. If it hadn't been for that crazy binocular strap catching on a sawed-off limb, she could have escaped without even a broken bone.

So he didn't feel that he could walk over to the officers and tell them the woman had been *murdered*. But he ought to tell them there had been somebody with her in the house, somebody who'd pushed her. There'd been something on one of the old Perry Mason reruns about a man who killed somebody, but he hadn't meant to, and they hadn't charged him with first degree murder . . . Rob tried to remember exactly what had happened on the show, but it got too mixed up with other shows in his mind.

Well, the thing to do was tell his father. *He'd* know what to do about it, if anything needed to be done.

6

Reluctantly, he made his way toward the small group beside the neighboring house. One of the officers, Riley, looked up and saw him.

"This the boy who saw it happen?"

"Yes, this is Rob. He was sitting in the tree . . . he often sits up there. He called us right away, but it was too late. By the time we got her down she was dead."

"Wouldn't be surprised if it broke her neck," the other officer commented, gesturing to the ambulance attendants who were hauling out their stretcher. "Kind of ironic, ain't it? I mean, she was the pest of the neighborhood with those binoculars, minding everybody else's business, and they're what killed her."

"You get complaints about her?" Mr. Mallory asked.

"Oh, not officially, not very often. But you hear things, a town the size of this one. *She* was always calling *us* about something. Somebody's dog, or kid, or something. Called us yesterday, said some young fella drove over her garden hose and wrecked it." He shook his head.

Max had overheard that. He strode toward them. "That was me. I didn't know she called the police. Her crummy hose was leaky already, and she left it in the street where I couldn't help running over it."

"Yeah. We figured that out, from what she said." Rob remembered the cop's name, now, the tall, skinny redhead with the big Adam's apple. Fritz. He didn't know if that was his last name or his first, but they called him Fritz. "Bit of a kook, wasn't she? Feuding with everybody all the time. I guess, living next door, you got the brunt of it?"

"Well, she wasn't an easy woman to live next to," Mr. Mallory admitted. They were all standing so they didn't have to look at Mrs. Calloway. Rob sneaked a look at her, felt his stomach lurch, and looked quickly away. Somehow he'd thought she'd stop looking so pop-eyed after they took her down. "She attacked Rob last night with a broom when he went over there to get our cat . . . and she enticed the cat by leaving meat scraps on the back porch."

Riley, the shorter, dark-haired one, nodded. "She was about ready to be committed, I guess. Maybe it's just as well this way, better for her than being locked up."

Rob cleared his throat. "Dad . . ."

"Later, son. I guess they're ready to take her away. I suppose there'll have to be an inquest?"

"Oh, yes, but there won't be any problem about it," Riley assured them. "It's perfectly clear what happened . . . and the boy saw it."

"He won't have to testify, will he? He's only eleven."

"I don't know for sure about that . . . it isn't up to us to decide . . . but I wouldn't worry about it, Walt. They won't make it any harder on him than they have to. What do you think, Fritz, we better get the crime lab out here? Take some pictures?"

"Well, it looks like an accident, pure and simple, but it wouldn't hurt to protect ourselves with a few pictures. Yeah, let's call in and let somebody else decide. You guys bring a sheet or something you can put over her? Whole blasted neighborhood's out gawking."

Rob hadn't noticed, but he did, now. People were coming out of their houses, leaning over the back fence, some of them even walking out across the lawns.

"Dad, when she fell . . ."

His father patted him on the shoulder. "Come on inside, son. The whole town's here, they don't need us. You want to use our telephone, Fritz?"

"No, I'll use the radio in the car. Go ahead inside. Be easiest if you came downtown, Walt . . . let somebody type up your statement."

"I don't have to do it today, I hope. My daughter's getting married tomorrow, and we've got a million things to do. Monday all right?"

"Well, if it isn't, we'll let you know. Somebody'll call you."

Rob was beginning to shake a little, he didn't know why. He had to trot to keep up with his father. "Dad, Mrs. Calloway didn't just fall out of the window . . ."

"Rob, let's not blow it up any bigger than it was, okay? I'd rather not get you involved in it at all. You had nothing to do with it, did you?"

"No, except I was . . . was spitting cherry pits at her window, and . . . and I guess that's why she leaned out the window."

Mr. Mallory gave him a tired grin. "Well, you ought to have known better than that, after everything else that's happened. But it didn't have anything to do with her hanging herself, you know. So try not to think about it."

"But there was somebody in there, Dad, I heard . . ." His words were wasted, uttered at the same moment his mother called from the window.

"Wally! Can you come to the phone? It's Jim French, and I told him you were awfully busy, but he said it's important. He sounds upset."

Mr. Mallory strode up the front steps and into the house, not hearing Rob's final words. Frustrated, Rob followed him, but his father was already on the telephone and his mother was saying, "Tell him to wait until Monday if it's business, honey. We've got too much to do to worry about anything else now."

Mr. Mallory made shushing gestures at her, speaking into the phone. "Yes, Jim, this is Walt."

It seemed to Rob that his father's face grew grim as he listened, although his mother didn't seem to notice anything. The doorbell rang, and she turned away to answer it.

Ellen Anderson stood there, a too-thin girl with long brown hair caught back in a ponytail with a rubber band.

"Hello, Mrs. Mallory. Darcy said I'd be doing her

64

a big favor if I could take Nancy's place in the wedding . . ."

"Yes, you will, if you can get into her dress."

"I think I can, but she's taller than I am, so it would have to be shortened."

"Maybe you could do that this afternoon."

"I don't know how to shorten anything, Mrs. Mallory. I flunked freshman sewing, and my mother just gave up on me."

"Maybe your mother . . ."

"My mother's gone to Kansas City for a week. My grandmother's sick."

Mrs. Mallory sighed. "Well, all right. Go up and try it on . . . it's in Darcy's room. I'll be up in a minute to pin it up."

Rob stood between his parents, feeling an urgent need to say something to one of them. They ought to know Mrs. Calloway was pushed out that window; surely it was important to let someone know that?

"Mom . . . I need to tell somebody . . ."

"Robbie, for heaven's sake, don't bother me now. I'm going to have to shorten that dress myself, obviously, unless I can get Aunt Grace to do it. Is she still here?"

"She's upstairs," Teddi volunteered, coming through the back of the house with a loaded tray.

"Where are you going with the refreshments?"

"For Darcy and Aunt Grace and me. Darcy says we won't have time to sit down for lunch."

The doorbell rang.

"Robbie, see who . . . Wally, where are you going?"

"I have to go see French. It's important, Marge; it

can't wait until Monday. I'll be back as soon as I can."

"What about the champagne? It has to be iced down . . ."

"Maybe you can find someone else to do it. Otherwise, I'll do it when I get back. Don't worry, I can pick it up any time up to midnight, honey. Rob, stay out of trouble and help your mother a little bit, will you?"

The doorbell rang again.

Mr. Mallory opened the door. "Oh, hi, Derek. Go on in, I'm just leaving. See you later."

Derek stood uncertainly just inside the doorway. "Mrs. Mallory?"

"Hello, Derek." Rob could see it when she remembered that his aunt had just died; the expression that crossed her face was a mixture of sympathy and reluctance to be the one to break the news.

"I thought maybe there was something I could do to help . . . run errands, or something."

"Derek . . . I appreciate the offer, and there are things . . . but maybe you'd ought to go home. The police . . . I mean, I think they'll have notified your mother by now, and . . ."

Derek stared at her. "The police? What are you talking about?"

"You haven't heard about your aunt, then. I'm sorry, I don't want to be the one to . . ."

Teddi, coming back down the stairs, paused on the bottom step. "I forgot the salt. Derek, haven't you had the radio on or anything? They just announced it on the radio."

"Announced what?" Derek's eyes swept across all

66

their faces, evaluating what he saw there. "Something's happened to Aunt Bea?"

"She's dead, Derek." Teddi descended the final step. "She fell out the window, and she's dead."

"From falling out her own window?" Derek asked.

"She was wearing those binoculars, and the strap caught on the limb of the cherry tree."

Derek swallowed. "She . . . hanged herself?"

"I guess so. Anyway, she's dead. The police and the ambulance took her away. Won't your mother need you at home, then? Will she be terribly upset?"

"She'll be in hysterics," Derek allowed. "Which means it's no place for me to be. Dad's home, he's not working today. Let him handle mother. I'd rather run errands than cope with that, if there's something I can do to make myself useful."

"Well, if you think it won't upset your family more . . ." Mrs. Mallory hesitated.

"I'd rather run errands," Derek repeated firmly.

"Well, Wally was supposed to pick up the champagne this afternoon. From Bullocks. There's room for part of it in the refrigerator at the Country Club, but the rest will have to be iced. We've got the cans, but someone has to pick up the ice, too."

"I'll be glad to do that for you, Mrs. Mallory." There were sounds overhead and Derek glanced up, no doubt hoping for a look at Darcy, but it was only Aunt Grace.

"Marge, that dress will have to be taken up about three inches to fit this girl. You want me to do it?" Aunt Grace asked, leaning over the railing.

"Yes, would you? That would be a tremendous

help. Here, Derek, I have the check written out to pay for the champagne, and I'll find some cash for the ice . . . oh, here's the key to get into the reception hall . . . it's for the back door."

Derek looked at Rob. "You want to come along and help, sport?"

Rob licked his lips. "I need to talk to Mom for a minute, first."

"Robbie, I don't have time to talk to you. Go on, you can help Derek handle the champagne. And while I think of it, did you get those spiders out of the living room?"

"No, not yet. I'll put them on the back porch."

His mother's voice was firm. "You get them completely out of the house, the way I told you. I don't want anyone coming across a jar full of spiders and being startled into a fit or something."

"But somebody might take them if I leave them around outside," Rob pointed out reasonably.

"I think that is most unlikely. Go on, help Derek or do something to make yourself useful."

He felt a slight stirring of resentment at the lack of sympathy in her tone. He didn't want to go with Derek. Derek was perfectly capable of hauling champagne by himself, Rob thought. He wanted to talk to someone . . . maybe Teddi would listen. Teddi usually listened, better than the rest of them.

"Oh. Well, all right, whatever you say." Derek hesitated, as if reluctant to leave. "What happened, exactly, about Aunt Bea? How did she come to fall out the window?"

"She was pushed," Rob said, and saw no change of expression in Derek's face.

"Oh, come on, Rob, that's not a thing to joke about."

"I'm not joking. I saw her."

"You saw someone push her out the window?" Derek was juggling keys, money, and the check, unbelieving. "Who did it?"

"I don't know. All I saw was his hands."

"A man? You saw a man's hands? What did they look like?"

With a growing sense of urgency, Rob tried to remember exactly how the hands had looked.

"I don't know. I only saw them for a minute . . . more like seconds, really, I guess. They were just . . . a man's hands!" He looked at Derek helplessly, shrugging.

"How did you know they were a man's hands? As opposed to a woman's?"

Derek wasn't the one he would have chosen to tell, but at least he was listening, more than anyone had done so far. Encouraged, Rob tried to be specific. "They were . . . too big to be a woman's. They were big, way bigger than mine." He spread his own fingers and stared at them for a minute, trying to see those other hands.

"Did they have hair all over them, or what? Dark hair, maybe?"

Rob searched his mind. "Not that I remember. No more than anybody's . . . Dad's, or yours, or . . ." A shadow loomed on the other side of the screen, and he looked that way. ". . . or Max's. Just hands."

Max saw him looking and opened the door for himself. "It's all right if I just walk in, isn't it? Your mother looks like she's ready to scream every time the

69

doorbell or the phone rings, so I hate to use them. Hello, Derek."

"Rob's been telling me something interesting. He says somebody pushed Aunt Bea out her window."

Max shook his head. "Honest to God, Rob, you've got a macabre sense of humor. You really have, kid. Where's Teddi?"

"Upstairs. What's macabre?"

"He means you aren't funny," Derek told him. "Listen, you coming with me after the champagne, or not?"

"No. You go on."

"I don't suppose you'd be interested, Max? In hauling the champagne over to the Country Club and icing it down? Mr. Mallory had to go somewhere."

Max shook his head. "No thanks, man. I'm hoping Teddi can cut loose from this madhouse sometime so we can get out for a few hours before the rehearsal. Is it safe to go up there, Rob?"

"I hate to guess, these days," Rob said. It was no use trying to tell anything to these two jerks. Maybe it wasn't really their fault, because he *had* told them some whoppers in the past. For the first time he could see the point to that stupid story about the boy who cried wolf. He'd never told them he'd seen anybody murdered before, though.

Max hesitated, looking up the stairs. "Hey, Teddi! You up there?"

She appeared on the upper landing, clad in a pale blue, full-skirted long dress. One of the bridesmaids' dresses, Rob knew. She looked quite un-Teddi-ish, even to Rob, with her hair caught back with a blue ribbon and a touch of lipstick on her mouth.

Max pursed his lips in a long drawn-out wolf whistle. "Hey, come on down, loverly, and let's see you!"

"No, I'm afraid to try the stairs in this. Darcy'd kill me if I stepped on the hem and tore it or broke my neck falling. But it's pretty, isn't it?"

"You're pretty," Max said and there was a different note in his voice. Rob recognized it with regret. Yep, old Darcy was moving on, but Teddi was going to take up where Darcy left off, with all the guys in town.

Teddi showed her dimples. "Wait a minute until I get it off, and I'll be down."

"Okay." Max turned to look at Derek. "I thought you were running off somewhere."

Still Derek hesitated. "I am. Only I thought it would be a help to have another pair of hands. I think I'm handling something like ten cases of champagne, if I heard Mr. Mallory right."

"Well, these hands are going to be otherwise engaged. Thanks for the invitation." Max put his hands in his pants pockets and walked into the living room, switching on the TV. Derek looked at Rob, who shook his head.

"See you later, Derek."

Derek muttered something under his breath, letting himself out the front door. It was quiet when he had gone. Rob licked his lips and made one more effort.

"Max . . . he made it sound funny, but it wasn't. It was true."

There was a cartoon show on the screen. Max flipped it off and straightened up. "What was true?"

"That I saw somebody push Mrs. Calloway . . ."

Max shook his head. "I'd have been tempted to

push her myself. I know you're not supposed to speak ill of the dead, but who can be sorry that old biddy has cashed in? No matter who moves into that house next door, it's got to be an improvement over her."

Momentarily diverted, Rob asked, "You think someone else will move in?"

"Well, not right away. They'll have to read her will, and it'll go through probate and all that jazz, and maybe it'll belong to Derek's mother, partly, anyway. Did she have any other relatives? They won't want it themselves, so they'll either rent it or sell it, more than likely. So somebody will live in it eventually."

"Max, would it be murder if somebody pushed her?"

Max regarded him casually. "Rob, you watch too much of the wrong kind of TV. Or maybe that's the only kind there is."

"No, I mean it. Would it be murder, if he didn't really intend to kill her? I mean, he couldn't have known the strap on the binoculars would catch on the tree, but you couldn't murder anybody by pushing them out a first floor window, could you?"

"If it was old Mrs. Calloway, I'd say the entire neighborhood would express its gratitude. Hey, you look good in ordinary clothes, too, girl."

It was no use. He couldn't get through to Max. He hadn't gotten very close even before Teddi showed up. There was no sense trying now; Max wasn't listening.

Teddi looked different, somehow, even back in her normal jeans and open-necked shirt.

"I don't dare go away," she told Max. "If Mom needs me, I have to be on call."

"I might have known you're only dangling the bait in front of me. You've no intention of letting me have a chance to bite it."

"I think there's a load of stuff to take over to the reception hall. Champagne glasses and paper plates and stuff like that. Can I tell Mom your car's available?"

"If you go along with the glasses and the paper plates," Max conceded. "So long, sport. Don't watch any more TV; it's bad for you."

And they were gone, and he hadn't had a chance to talk to Teddi, either. Ordinarily, he'd have been sure Teddi would listen. But after seeing her just now, the way she was turning on the sparkle for old Max, Rob thought in discouragement, he wasn't sure of anything.

7

He fixed himself something to eat and fed S.O.B., whose breakfast had been lost in the shuffle. The cat ate greedily, crouched over the plastic dish on the kitchen floor.

He wondered how his father was coming with Mr. French, if he'd managed to calm him down. Mr. French must have discovered his money was missing. Rob wondered, idly, what his Uncle Ray had done with twelve hundred dollars. It seemed like an awful lot of money.

But mostly he wondered how he was ever going to convince anyone that he wasn't kidding about Mrs. Calloway being pushed out the window. He wasn't sure how important it was, but it seemed as if someone ought to know, someone beside himself.

After one salami sandwich and one tuna fish one, which he grudgingly shared with S.O.B., he dished up some ice cream and poured chocolate syrup over it, adding a sliced banana as an afterthought, and carried it out onto the back steps. The more he thought about it, the more interesting it was.

Who had the man been, in there with Mrs. Calloway? She almost never had company. She was Derek's great-aunt, but Derek hadn't liked her any better than anybody else did, and he only went there when his mother made him deliver something. Derek's mother never came at all.

The neighbors, all of them, hated her. Because the Mallorys lived next door, they had more trouble with her than the others; but there wasn't a family within two blocks in each direction that hadn't had some problem with her at one time or another. She was always calling the police on somebody; not that the cops came, usually, but sometimes they would. They'd stand on the curb and explain that the old lady was complaining about whatever it was, and they'd roll their eyes toward her house, and ask if people wouldn't try to stay away from her.

Everybody did try, really. Only it was hard to know how to stop a cat from walking across her precious grass, or the wind from blowing a garbage can lid into her yard, or to keep the sounds down when she wanted to sleep in the middle of the day. Three different times she'd called the police to arrest Mr. Dunbarton for disturbing the peace when he ran his power saw in the afternoon.

Once she went around yelling and making threats when Mrs. Bond, whose property faced Mrs. Calloway's across the alley, sprayed some sort of insecticide and it drifted across the way and killed some of Mrs. Calloway's bugs. She said it would kill the birds, too. Boy, that had been a battle and a half!

He ate the ice cream slowly; it was good. S.O.B. had come with him and was squatting on the bottom step against one foot.

So who was it, then, in the house with the old lady just before she died?

Pretty soon, if they all kept making fun of him, he'd begin to think himself that he'd imagined it.

He knew he hadn't, though. There had been a man in there, and he'd been angry enough to push the old woman out the window.

She'd said something, just before she fell, Rob remembered. What was it? He paused, trying to pin it in his mind.

She'd looked at the cherry pits and said something about a nasty little boy . . . meaning him, of course. And then she'd said . . . "You must be out of your mind to think I'd agree to any such thing."

He thought about that, unable to imagine what that remark had been in reply to. Then he backed up his memory just a bit further, to when she had first come to the window.

"I will not," she had said, and her voice had been hard and stubborn. The way it usually was.

Whoever he was in there, he'd wanted her to do something. Something she refused to do, and she made the man so angry he'd shoved her. Not thinking to kill her, probably, but just so mad he couldn't help himself.

It wasn't hard to imagine someone being that mad at her. What was hard was thinking of anyone who'd go into her house and ask her for anything.

He scraped the last of the ice cream out of the

76

bottom of his dish and licked off his lips. He got up to take the dish back into the house and heard the telephone ringing. At the same time, the doorbell sounded.

His mother stood in the middle of the kitchen, looking upset.

"Robbie, go see who's at the door. I'll get the phone. Where's Teddi, do you know?"

"She went with old Max, to take some stuff over to the Country Club."

"Oh. I'm coming, I'm coming!" she said to the phone, and reluctantly Rob moved toward the front door. Behind him he heard his mother's quick "Hello?" and then her low wail of protest. "Oh, Wally! Why? What for? . . . Well, I suppose if you *have* to . . . You'll be here for dinner, won't you? Don't forget rehearsal is at 7:30, and Darcy's counting on you for that . . ."

From that he gathered that his father wasn't going to be right home, then. What had Mr. French decided? Were they sending the police after Uncle Ray? He wondered if they'd go with their sirens screaming and arrest him and then the police would come and tell his mother her brother was in jail . . .

No, he decided, scuffing his feet through the shag carpeting, they wouldn't tell *her*. His grandmother, maybe, because Ray lived with her. Or would they tell anybody at all? Wasn't that what the one phone call you were allowed was for? So you could notify whoever you wanted?

He guessed his father would try to find Uncle Ray before the police did. That was supposed to be better,

77

wasn't it, if you turned yourself in? He wondered, if Uncle Ray resisted arrest, if they'd shoot him. He hoped not. His mother would be very upset, even if it didn't spoil the wedding.

There was a delivery man at the door. He thrust a clipboard at Rob. "Sign here, please. Line twelve."

Rob signed. "What is it?"

"Wedding presents, I guess. Somebody getting married?"

"My sister."

The delivery man nodded. "Where you want me to put this stuff? There's quite a bit of it."

The only downstairs bedroom had been filling with gifts over the past weeks. Rob showed him where it was, and the man carried in box after box. Darcy peered over the stair railing.

"Are those for me, Rob?"

"I guess so. They're all boxes from The China and Glass Shoppe."

His mother had disappeared somewhere, maybe back upstairs. Rob hesitated, wondering if there was any point in trying to talk to Darcy.

He and Darcy had never been very close. Still, she was coming downstairs and there wasn't anyone else around, so maybe it was worth a try.

She moved past him into the bedroom, pouncing on the packages. "Dozens of them! I wonder if I ought to open this batch now? I wish Steve was here . . . it's as good as Christmas. When your time comes and they try to talk you into eloping, Robbie, don't listen to them. You don't get wedding gifts like this if you elope."

He stood in the doorway, watching as his sister opened an envelope and then, making up her mind, began to unwrap a white-and-silver-papered box.

"Darcy."

"Oh, wow! Look, isn't it beautiful?"

"Yeah, I guess." He didn't even look at what it was. "Darcy, listen. I keep trying to tell somebody, but nobody listens. It's about Mrs. Calloway."

"Darling, don't talk about Mrs. Calloway. I'm sorry she got hanged, but I don't intend to let it spoil my wedding. It's not as if she was a friend or anything like that. I'd rather not think about her at all, Rob, please."

The telephone rang.

"Get that, will you, Robbie? If it's Steve, I want to talk to him."

Reluctantly, Rob answered the phone. If Steve came over, maybe he'd listen. Steve was pretty sensible, except where Darcy was concerned. With her, he was as bad as the rest of them.

"Hiya, Robbie? Steve. Any chance of talking to my girl, or has she succumbed to the pressures?"

"She's opening presents. They just delivered a half truckload of 'em."

"Great! Let me talk to her, huh?"

He met his mother in the hall. "Rob, what is that ungodly smell in your bedroom?"

"What smell? I have to call Darcy, it's Steve . . ."

"It smells like something's died up there."

"Was it for me, Rob?" Darcy poked her head out of the bedroom. "Oh, hi, Mom. It looks like I've got nine place settings of my china, and eight of the crystal! Isn't that marvelous! Was it Steve, Rob?"

"Yes." He stepped aside so his sister could get to the phone in the study. His mother was bearing down on him in a way that made him uneasy.

"Rob, whatever's making that odor, you've got to get rid of it! I'll get air freshener up there and I've already opened all the windows, but I can't possibly put anyone in there to sleep the way it is! Go find whatever it is and get it out of there."

"I didn't notice anything."

"Well, I did, and so did Aunt Grace. And you'd better find another place for that junk under the bed. Haven't you any room in your closet?"

"It's handier under the bed," Rob said, but without much force. She looked about ready to hit him, and while she hadn't done that for a long time, he wouldn't rule out the possibility. "Maybe whatever stinks is Randolph; he's been missing for a few days. He got loose."

"Well, whatever it is, find it and then scrub the spot where it's been. I hope to heaven we can get the odor out of there by evening or I don't know what I'll do."

Randolph was a mouse. He'd traded an old pair of skates for him, and then the darned mouse had disappeared the second day he had him. Gloomily, Rob tramped upstairs.

When he got to his room, he *could* smell something. Very faintly, however; nothing to get all excited about. He stood in the middle of the floor, wondering where Randolph would have gone to die. That Paddy Wilson, the crumb had probably known the mouse was sick or something when he traded him.

It took him ten minutes to find Randolph; he had crawled into the back part of the bookcase, behind some books. Up close, he had a rotten smell, indeed. Rob scooped him up on a piece of cardboard, briefly considered putting him in a matchbox to return to Paddy, and then decided the smell was strong enough so there was no place he could expect to conceal the creature until Monday, which would be the soonest he could get to Paddy. Reluctantly, he flushed Randolph down the toilet.

He scooped the stuff out from under the bed . . . nothing to make a big fuss over, it was just a football and helmet and some rocks he was saving . . . and crammed them into the closet. Now maybe they'd leave him alone. It would help, too, if he could get someone to listen to what he had to say about Mrs. Calloway.

His aunt was in his parents' bedroom, hemming. She had the dress laid out across the foot of the king-sized bed and was working on it. She looked up when she saw him, her mouth tightening.

"Did you get rid of that stink in your bedroom?"

"Yes." He considered. Was it worth trying to talk to her? He had never had much to do with his Aunt Grace, she didn't like him. His father said it was because she'd raised only girls and had no concept of what a normal boy was like.

Still, it didn't matter what she thought of boys, did it? The important thing was that someone ought to know about Mrs. Calloway. Rob paused in the doorway.

"Don't get against this dress," she warned, although he was a good five feet from it and couldn't possibly have damaged it. "One more catastrophe is about all we need."

"Aunt Grace . . . is it murder to push somebody out a window, if it's not very high off the ground? I mean, nobody'd think it would kill anybody . . . only if it does . . ."

She grimaced with distaste. "Good grief, you do have a morbid turn of mind, don't you? It's allowing you to watch all that television without any super-vision . . . horrid things they put on nowadays. I've told Marge it isn't good for you."

"It's not on TV, it's Mrs. Calloway. She was . . ."

"Rob, run along. You're distracting me, and I want to hurry and finish this. It's a mile around, I swear, and it's making me nervous, all this last-minute rush."

"But I need . . ."

Her voice cut firmly through his. "Go along, do as I tell you. I don't like talking about such gruesome things; it's enough to give a civilized person night-mares. You might tell someone I'd appreciate a cup of tea, if they have time to fix it."

He left then. There was little point in trying to talk to her.

Maybe it didn't matter if he didn't talk to anyone before his father got back. It would only be a few hours, and he knew his father would listen to him if he once got his mind off Uncle Ray going to jail or whatever they were going to do. His father didn't think he was morbid or gruesome; even his mother wouldn't ordinarily flip out over a simple thing like asking if something was murder.

The doorbell rang as he was going down the stairs. He wondered if his mother would kill him if he disconnected it. But it wouldn't do any good, anyway. Whoever it was pounded on the doorframe, then pushed on into the house without waiting for it to be answered.

"Well, hi, there, Rob boy! Where is everybody? We're all here, safe and sound! Didn't want to miss little Darcy's wedding, so we brought the whole family. Shall we bring our bags inside?"

Rob caught the expression on his mother's face before the others saw her; she obviously wasn't happy. Well, it was her own fault. Who invited them?

"Sylvester! We didn't expect you so early!"

"Oh, we got a good early start. Didn't want to miss out on anything. Shall we bring our bags in, Marge?"

There seemed to be dozens of them. Mrs. Mallory must have been making her own count, because she said with only a slight tremor in her voice, "Who all came?"

"Oh, the whole family, and we stopped in Studeville and picked up Elsie and Rich and little Neddy. They wasn't planning to come because their car was broke down, but we had to bring two cars anyway, so we told them we had plenty of room."

His mother was looking rather pale, Rob thought, but she was welcoming them all. He withdrew as quickly as he could toward the back of the house, before any of them should decide to kiss him or something. Now *that* was *his* idea of gruesome.

He didn't know Sylvester or the others very well, although they sometimes came over the Christmas holidays. Then they usually stayed with his Grandmother Mallory, and he hadn't liked any of them well enough to try to get better acquainted. Little Neddy he remembered; he'd pulled up all his mother's tulips the last time he was here, and broken a vase she especially valued.

He didn't want to stick around long enough to get caught up with that crowd, and he knew he'd better remove the spiders before Aunt Sylvia saw them, or his cousin Elsie. Elsie was grown up, but she was a real fraidy cat. He got the jar and held it so nobody would notice what was in it, and on his way past the hall table he rescued two small vases so that they'd be out of reach of three-year-old hands. He put them on the windowsill in the kitchen.

S.O.B. immediately jumped up to investigate them, and Rob cuffed him sharply. "You knock those off, stupid, and they're apt to draw and quarter you!"

S.O.B. withdrew with dignity, gazing at him through resentful yellow eyes.

"And if I were you," Rob went on in a conversational tone, "I'd stay out of the way of Neddy. I'll bet he picks cats up by their necks."

S.O.B. switched his tail in a challenging manner.

"Yeah, well, you scratch the little brat, even if he is choking you to death, and his mother will kill you."

"Who are you talking to?"

His Aunt Grace had come down for her tea, since no one had brought it up. She looked around the empty kitchen.

"Just S.O.B."

"Where's your mother keep the tea?"

He found it for her, silently. She nearly stepped on S.O.B., who stood his ground; he knew his rights. He made a protesting sound when Rob scooped him up and put him out on the porch. Aunt Grace wasn't terribly fond of cats, either.

"Oh, Marge . . . I'm just making myself some tea. Do you want some?"

"What I really need," Mrs. Mallory said frankly, "is a very dry martini. Which I don't dare have. Grace, did you see that mob they brought? Sylvester and nine other people! Where am I going to put them? Does Mother have any sleeping space left?"

"No. Every corner is filled. Unless Ray's gone . . . his room would be empty."

"Ray? Is he gone somewhere?" Mrs. Mallory paused, frowning, in the act of reaching for a cup. "Isn't he going to be here for the wedding?"

Nobody was paying any attention to Rob. He heard Aunt Grace start to pick up the pieces on that blooper. It would be good to see how she got out of that, but it also seemed a good time to slip out the back door with his spiders. He put them down in the grass beside the steps until he could think of a safe place for them. They moved sluggishly, climbing over one another.

It was pleasantly hot in the sunshine. Rob picked at one of the scabs on his lip and started the place bleeding again. S.O.B. came to crouch beside him, rubbing against his leg. Rob put down a hand to stroke the dark fur, feeling the powerful muscles beneath it. It wouldn't be a bad life, to be a cat like S.O.B.

Something hit the step between his feet with a sharp, splintering sound.

Rob glanced down, frowning, and saw that a bit of

the wood had been torn away. There was a second report, and S.O.B. screamed in pain and fury, bounding away toward a refuge in the shrubbery.

Unbelieving, Rob sat for a moment more, staring at the drops of blood left in a trail across the concrete of the sidewalk. He dove after the cat at last, only vaguely aware of the third shell that hit the porch steps right where he had been sitting.

8

He hauled the protesting cat out of the bushes and ran his hands over the animal. At least he wasn't killed, though he easily might have been. At first Rob couldn't even find where the blood was coming from, and then his fingers felt moisture.

"Robbie! Robbie, was that someone shooting?"

His mother came to the door, her voice anxious.

"Some dumb kid shooting a .22, I think."

She saw the blood then. Not a lot of it, but enough so you could tell what it was. "Robbie, were you hit?"

"No, they got S.O.B., though. It's just on his tail . . . scared him more than anything, I guess." He carried the big cat toward the house. "I hope it didn't break it . . . do you think it did?"

Anger swept across her face. "What's the matter with anybody who'd shoot right into someone's yard? Who around here has a .22?"

"Oh, practically everybody, Mom. What'll I do with S.O.B.?"

Surprisingly, S.O.B. allowed her to examine him.

Usually he hated being touched by anyone but Rob, unless he asked to be petted. Mrs. Mallory parted the hair, examining the area at the base of his tail.

"No, I don't think it's broken. I don't think we have to do anything to it; he'll take care of it himself. But that idiot might have killed S.O.B. . . . or you, for that matter, if you were right here, too. I've got a good mind to call the police."

He remembered his father's comments about calling the police when Mrs. Calloway had attacked him.

"Are you sure you want to take time to talk to the police? They come around writing out reports and everything."

"Well . . . I suppose I haven't got any time to spare, but if it happens again, I'll have to make the time before someone gets hurt. Did you find what was smelling up your room?"

"Yes. It was Randolph, like I thought. He's gone now. I think I'll punch that Paddy in the mouth. I'll bet he knew that mouse was going to die."

"Give him the benefit of the doubt, and forget it. You don't need to be any more battered than you are already."

"Paddy's so fat, he can't lay a hand on me."

"Then it's hardly fair to hit him, is it?"

"It wasn't fair to trade me a sick mouse, either."

"You can't be sure he knew it was sick. Robbie, run up and dig out those old sleeping bags, will you? We're going to need them all, I guess, and then I'm not sure we'll have enough to go around."

"Dad already got them out. They're on the upper landing."

"Just the good ones. We're going to need the older ones, too. And I think yours is still in your closet. Maybe Neddy could sleep in that."

Rob looked at her in dismay. "Mom, Neddy wets his/pants!"

"Well, if he ruins your bag, we'll replace it. You need a new one, anyway. Go on, please, get the others out. I'm going out of my mind trying to think where to put everyone."

"Didn't you invite them all?"

"Yes, but most of them said they couldn't come, so I told Nick he could sleep here as well as Sylvia and Sylvester. We'll have to move you out of your own room . . . Lord knows where you'll find a few feet of floor space to spread a sleeping bag. Oh, and we'll have to move the wedding presents off the bed in the spare room. There's no place to put them if we're going to use the dining room, so people will just have to climb around them, but get everything moved off the bed, at least, will you?"

He knew it had been a mistake not to vanish when he'd had the chance. He put the cat down, and S.O.B. streaked along the house, retreating to a hideaway underneath where no one could get at him. Rob didn't blame him. If he could think of a place to go, he'd hide, too.

His mother had turned to go back into the house; she paused with one final order. "Oh, and move the sprinkler, will you? Be sure to keep the water off the sidewalks."

Cripes, if he lived through this weekend it would be a miracle. Rob turned off the water, plodded through the wet grass to pick up the sprinkler, and moved it closer to Mrs. Calloway's house. It was going to be funny to think of it as somebody else's house.

He could make out the crushed spot on the grass where the old woman's body had been before they took it away. The men had walked in her flowerbeds, too, crushing some geraniums. He could just hear her now, up in heaven, giving them what-for, for trampling her flowers.

Wow, what was he thinking? Old Lady Calloway wasn't going to be in heaven, was she? If she got there, *he* sure didn't want to join her.

He couldn't remember afterward why he had suddenly moved away from the house. Maybe he'd heard some sound from above, he didn't know. Just standing where the body had been . . . the corpse, he thought . . . was enough to give a guy the creeps. He jumped right in the nick of time, anyway, for whatever reason.

The pot landed where he had been moments earlier. With a sickening crack the container split on a rock that edged a flower bed, forming two halves with the dirt and some scroungy-looking plant remaining intact between the sections.

Rob stood quite still, looking at it, then gazing upward to where it must have fallen from. He didn't think the old lady had been upstairs in years, yet she must have, because there was a window open. Right over his head. Funny place to keep a plant, when you spent most all your time on the ground floor. He scowled at it. As a matter of fact, it looked like one of the plants she'd kept on the rail on the back porch.

Cripes, the thing could have killed him if he'd still been standing there. He wondered what had made it fall.

Well, it hadn't hit him. He shrugged, kicking at the dirt so that it came apart. It wasn't rock-hard, like dirt that hadn't been watered lately. He kicked the pottery pieces into the flower bed beside the house and then glanced around, guiltily. If anybody saw him and thought he'd broken it on purpose, they'd be sort of ticked off.

Just out of curiosity, he walked toward the back of the house to look at the row of pots on the porch rail. There were five of them, just like the one that had fallen from the second story. Had there been six, when he was lying out there smeared with catsup, waiting for Mrs. Calloway to find him?

He couldn't remember. It didn't matter, anyway. He crossed to his own yard and turned on the water, setting the sprinkler to whirling.

Across the street he saw Paddy and Bo Crepps and Andy Dunbarton. They were wearing bathing trunks and carrying towels over their shoulders, off to the city pool. He wished he could go, too; it would be a lot more fun than hauling out sleeping bags and dodging little Neddy, but he knew it was pointless to ask. His mother would probably froth at the mouth if he even mentioned it. He sure hoped she'd get back to normal immediately after this blamed wedding was over. Well, as soon as all the relatives went home, anyway.

Old Max's car drew up at the curb as he rounded the corner of the house. Teddi looked bright and happy. There must be something different about girls;

they all seemed to love weddings, no matter whose they were or how much bother.

"Hi, Rob! Who all's here?" She pointed to the station wagon full of luggage and the dusty sedan behind it.

He told her. "And Neddy. Nasty little Neddy."

"Oh, he's only a baby, Rob. He's all right."

"Last time he was here he wet in the middle of my bed. Now Mom wants to put him in my sleeping bag tonight."

"Oh, probably they'll put plastic pants on him, or something. He's cute. Your mouth's bleeding."

He touched it with a finger, which came away smeared with red. "I guess I picked at the scab."

"You'd better stop that. Darcy's having fits now about the way you're going to spoil her wedding pictures. It's a good thing you aren't an usher or ring-bearer or anything, so you'd have to be in the official pictures."

Max grinned at him. "She'd have you painted up with makeup to cover the black eyes and the scabs. You really are a thing of beauty, mate."

"I pretty nearly was even worse." He told them about the falling flowerpot. "And before that some nut with a .22 fired into the yard. Didn't hit me, I was sitting on the back steps, but it got S.O.B.'s tail and made it bleed."

Teddi's concern showed on her face. "Did you take him to the vet's?"

"No. Mom said he could take care of it himself. He's hiding under the house."

"I'd hide under the house, too," Max approved.

"Boy, this is one swinging neighborhood today. Listen, Teddi, do you think there's any chance of ripping off a beer and a sandwich before we take on the next project? I'm about to perish of starvation."

"Sure. Come on in."

Rob watched them go. Good old helpful Max. He bet if Teddi wasn't here he wouldn't be around offering to run errands.

"Catch me doing a lot of unnecessary work because of some dumb girl," he muttered, and went to get down the sleeping bags.

He had to get into his closet for his own, and he found his cousin Elsie there, putting little Neddy down for a nap on his own bed. Rob halted with the rolled sleeping bag hugged against his chest, looking at the child.

He didn't see what was cute about him. Anybody could tell he was a stinker, just looking into his big blue eyes. He wondered why they didn't cut his hair; all those yellow curls, he looked like a girl.

"Last time he wet on my bed," Rob said.

Elsie smiled at him. "Oh, he doesn't do that anymore, do you, honey? Don't worry, Robbie, he won't wet."

"He'd better not. I just put clean sheets on the bed, and Mom says we're running out of sheets."

His cousin smiled reassuringly. "Don't worry. Neddy's a big boy now."

Obviously nothing he said was going to make a difference. Rob left, adding his own sleeping bag to the stack on the landing. Be lucky if he had a place to sleep himself tonight.

He almost ran into Derek in the lower hallway. He thought Derek looked tired, like maybe hauling that champagne was hard work.

"Oh, hi, Rob. I wondered where you were."

"Why?"

Derek gave him an odd look. "Well, why not? I mean, everybody else is around."

"Dad's not."

"Oh? Well, it doesn't matter. I need to talk to your mother, actually. Do you know where she is?"

"No. She's not upstairs, I know that."

Derek followed him toward the rear of the house. "Who are all the people running in and out?"

"Relatives."

"Are they all staying here? Where you going to put them?"

Rob didn't answer. Teddi and Max and his mother were all in the kitchen; Max had a can of beer, and Teddi was making sandwiches.

"Hey, that looks good. I don't suppose you've got another one?" Derek asked.

Mrs. Mallory turned with a smile, looking almost her normal self. "Teddi, get the boy a beer. You want a sandwich, too?"

"No, thanks. I had some trouble, Mrs. Mallory."

Rob edged over to the counter. "Is there enough tuna fish so I can have some, too?"

Mrs. Mallory's smile had faded. "What sort of trouble?"

"Well, with my car. It stalled. I got stranded a few blocks away. It won't start. It's the fuel pump, I think. I'll have to go get a new one. I picked up the champagne, okay, but I still have it in the car. I couldn't get it over to the Country Club."

"And the ice?"

"I didn't get the ice yet."

"Give me a chance to ease my hunger pangs, and I'll relieve you of the champagne and go get the ice," Max offered. "If Teddi can be spared to come along and direct things?"

Mrs. Mallory sighed. "Yes, I guess so. Grace got that dress hemmed, and I think I've got beds figured out; pray nobody else shows up at the last minute. Listen, you kids are on your own for food until after the rehearsal. I don't know what to do about the mob that showed up . . . I hadn't planned dinner for so many."

"Send them out to Colonel Sanders," Teddi suggested.

"Maybe that's what we'd better do. Pick up some chicken and some more salads from the delicatessen, and that ought to stretch it. Maybe Max? . . ."

"Sure, I'll go pick it up for you." Max stuck his head into the refrigerator and got himself another beer. "Hey, that looks good enough to be eaten twice!"

Teddi made a face at him. "Is that a polite way of saying you want two of them?"

Rob made his own sandwich and started for the back door. Eating outdoors was easier than watching where all the bits of lettuce fell.

"You want to come along and help us transfer the champagne to Max's car?" Derek called after him.

"No, thanks." He escaped to the comparative peace of the yard. Just before he sat down on the steps,

95

though, he remembered that's where he'd been when that nut fired off the .22. He hesitated, then sank down, probing the splintered spot with one finger. He hadn't heard any more firing, so the kid must have gone somewhere else. Maybe he'd realized how close he came to hitting someone.

He chewed on the sandwich, idly figuring out the probable trajectory of the .22 shell. His frown deepened as he thought he had it located . . . but it wasn't very likely anyone had fired from upstairs in Mrs. Calloway's house.

The idea, when it came, was startling enough to make him stop eating.

What if it *had* been fired from there? When he got to thinking about it, where else *could* it have come from, to hit where it did, at the angle it did?

The sun was hot on his bare arms, but Rob felt a sudden chill, like somebody'd run cold water down his spine.

What if it wasn't some stupid kid, at all, but somebody shooting at *him*?

9

Rob tried to shrug it off, it was so fantastic, but the idea nagged at him. That heavy pot, too, falling from a part of the house where he didn't think anybody ever went any more. It had come from that front window on this side, and the shot could have been fired from there, too.

He'd lost his appetite. He put the remains of the tuna sandwich down on a step where S.O.B. would find it and sat looking at the house next door.

After a few minutes he got up and slowly made his way toward the Calloway house, the back part of it. He walked right up on the porch, his heart pounding so it ought to have made his shirt stick out with the force of it, although he knew that was silly. The old witch was dead and carried off; she couldn't hurt him. And if there was anybody up on the second floor, they couldn't possibly see him or do anything to him while he was back here.

The flowerpots sat in a row on the white-painted railing. Five of them. And there was a mark where the sixth one had sat, right on the end. It was easy to see, because there was a cleaner spot which had been covered by the pot and then stains where the water had leaked through it.

Somebody took that pot upstairs. Why?

To drop on me, he thought, and knew what all those people at home would say if he sprung that on them. They'd all bring up his macabre turn of mind, his morbid sense of humor, his poor taste.

He was sweating heavily, although it wasn't really so hot there on the porch. He stood for a moment, not really wanting to make the return trip across the yard to his own house.

"Hey, Rob! What're you doing?"

Derek stood on the Mallory steps, watching him.

Rob relaxed a little. It wouldn't be smart of anybody to try to . . . to shoot him, or anything, with a witness standing by, would it? He went down the steps and walked toward Derek.

"I was just . . . checking something out."

"Yeah? What?"

"Oh, nothing special. What will happen now to the house, do you think?"

"I don't know. I suppose my mother will get it. Why? You want to live in it?"

Rob couldn't repress a shiver. "No, I never want to go in it."

"Oh, I don't know. She had a lot of junk over there, but I guess there's some stuff that's valuable, too. It's a big, roomy house. A family with twelve kids would have plenty of space. Too bad some of it isn't available for this crowd your mother has now. Are you going to have enough sleeping space for everybody?"

"I guess so. Mom's got it figured out."

"We've got one extra room. If you want to get away from that little kid, what's his name? Neddy? Why don't you come over and stay with us tonight?"

"No, thanks. I can sleep on the floor like everybody else."

"Well, suit yourself. If you change your mind when you find out you have to sleep with six other people, let me know."

Max came out of the house, eating a piece of cake. "'Ready to go? You coming, Rob?"

"No. Is that cake up for grabs?"

"Far as I know. See you later, then."

They went off together, and Rob went in and got himself a wedge of cake. Nothing had happened when he was outside this time. Nothing at all. Was he just letting his imagination run away with him? His family all said he tended to do that. Maybe he did, but he knew when he was pretending and when he wasn't. He sure hadn't pretended either the shots or the falling flowerpot.

If somebody had tried to get him . . . there had to be a reason. He bit into the cake which was moist and chocolatey, chewing slowly. He watched enough television to figure out the answer to that. A guy got shot at because somebody wanted to be rid of him . . . he knew something he wasn't supposed to know, he'd seen something he shouldn't have seen.

There was only one thing he knew about that maybe he shouldn't have. That was Mrs. Calloway's death. That was hearing somebody talking to her . . . well,

hearing her talk to somebody else . . . and then seeing those arms pushing her out of the window.

He forgot about the taste of the cake, chewing
mechanically. Had she really been murdered? Had
somebody not just pushed her because he was mad
at what she'd said to him, but because he wanted to
kill her?

He thought about it a little more, pouring a glass
of milk to balance the cake. If those things did happen
because of what he'd seen from the cherry tree, then
the sooner he told somebody . . . everybody . . .
about it, the safer he'd be.

Only who was he going to tell? Who could he get
to listen?

He'd make one more try with his mother, he decided.

He found her in the spare bedroom, supervising
sleeping arrangements for Sylvester and Sylvia. There
were some six people in the room, besides Marge, shifting wedding presents, opening and unpacking luggage,
talking and getting in one another's way.

He had to raise his voice to be heard over the
tumult.

"Mom, I have to talk to you."

"Not now, Rob, I want to get people squared away
here so they all know where they're sleeping. So the
kids can go to bed when they get tired, whether I'm
around then to give instructions or not."

"But it's important, Mom. It's practically a matter
of life and death."

"So's this. Please, Rob, don't be a pest. It isn't like
you to deliberately irritate me when you know I'm

already frantic. Why don't you go up and keep an eye on Neddy? He's sleeping, and he may be frightened if he wakes up in a strange place."

"Mom, honest, it's real important. It'll only take a minute . . ."

"A minute is something I haven't got." She didn't notice the urgency in his tone; she was scarcely even looking at him. "Go on, look in on Neddy. When this is over, we'll have plenty of time to talk."

Serve her right if somebody murdered me before then, Rob thought, anger rising. *Only trouble is, I don't want to take the chance.*

He climbed the stairs, stepping aside for a crowd of giggling girl cousins on the way down, reaching the upper landing in a foul humor.

It was like one of those dumb old Abbott and Costello movies, where it was really important to tell someone something and totally impossible to do it. It looked funny on the screen, but he didn't see any humor in it now.

He eased open the door to his room and stopped, outraged. Neddy wasn't sleeping at all; he was standing on the bed, taking apart the model of the *Constitution* that had taken him days to assemble. Not to mention that he'd spent two weeks' allowance on it.

"You little brat! Give me that!" Rob snatched at the remains, knowing already that it was too late. He'd never be able to fix it. He heard some of the parts crunching under his own feet.

Neddy opened his mouth and let out a blood-curdling shriek; he fought for the damaged hulk.

Rob was stronger, and force won out as he twisted

the model out of Neddy's hands; in so doing, he up-set Neddy's balance and he fell off the bed, striking his head against the corner of the dresser.

The sound Neddy uttered this time was no bellow of rage but a genuine cry of pain. Rob stared at him, uncertain what to do next. Cripes, why couldn't they have put him to bed somewhere else?

Elsie came running into the room, scooping up her child, then whirling on Rob with a fury that astounded him.

"How could you! He's only a baby, how could you hurt him this way?"

"I didn't hurt him. I only took my model away from him. He wrecked it."

"Look at his head! You ought to be ashamed of yourself, a great big boy like you!"

"I didn't do anything to him. He fell off the bed. I never touched him."

"What on earth . . . is he all right?" Mrs. Mallory stood in the doorway, looking from Rob's pale face to the two flushed ones. "What happened?"

Rob started to explain but Elsie got there first. "He knocked poor Neddy on the floor! Look at the lump on his head! Poor baby, don't cry, Neddy!"

"I didn't," Rob said, tight-lipped. "I never touched him. I only took my ship model away from him, and he fell off the bed by himself."

"A great big boy like you," Elsie said accusingly. "You ought to be ashamed."

"Rob, he *is* only a baby . . ." Mrs. Mallory began.

It was all so stupid. They could see Neddy had wrecked the model, and there was no reason to think he'd pushed the kid. Why wouldn't they listen? He said it aloud.

"Why won't anybody listen to me? Why won't anybody shut up long enough to hear my side of anything?" He had said it too loudly; he knew that at once by their expressions, although at last Elsie had stopped accusing him. She compressed her lips, and carried Neddy out of the room.

Mrs. Mallory looked at him with some coolness.

"You're being very rude, to shout that way, Rob."

He tried to keep his voice under control, but he couldn't. He was hurt and angry and, yes, scared, and he couldn't sound calm and unconcerned. "Why won't you listen to me, then? I keep trying to *tell* you, and all you can think about is that stupid Neddy! It was his own fault he hurt himself, it served him right for wrecking my model! *She* was screaming, Neddy was screaming, and the only way anybody could hear me was if I yelled, too!"

"I'm not yelling," his mother pointed out, "but you still are. With a houseful of company . . . I hate to imagine what they're thinking about you, Rob."

He was not going to cry. No matter how mad he was, he wasn't going to cry, but his eyes stung. "What do I have to do to get you to listen to me? Nobody will even listen, and its important . . ." Somewhere in the house something fell and smashed; Darcy's wail of anguish drew his mother further away from him.

He saw her face close. As if a door had been shut, right in front of him.

"That's enough, Rob. Your theatrics are all right when it's just family at home, when we have time to

103

make them fun. But this isn't fun, and you're not amusing me in the slightest. This has been one of the worst days I can remember, and if you don't shut up right this minute, I'm going to lose my temper and slap you!"

He stared at her, trembling all over now, and he thought sure she would have to see how upset he was if she were looking right at him. Instead she was already moving to see which of the wedding presents had been broken. With a supreme effort, choking on it, he brought his voice to a very low level, very soft, very quiet.

"Mom, I'm not kidding, I'm not trying to be funny. Somebody is trying to . . ."

He thought she was really going to hit him. Her hand started to move in the beginning motions, and then she spoke with a deadly coldness he had never known in her before. "All right. If that's the way you want it. But I'm not going to put up with it, and nobody else will have to, either. You can stay in your room until you decide to behave yourself and apologize to Elsie."

She was gone, closing the door with considerable force, leaving him alone.

The trembling was out of control, now; he had to sit down. He did so, on the edge of his own bed, and found that it was wet. Neddy had wet the bed.

The tears came then, and he couldn't stop them. Blinding, hot, angry tears. He wiped at them frantically, smearing his face. He got up, feeling the broken bits of the *Constitution* underfoot. He kicked at them, savagely, saying the worst swear word he knew. He wasn't sure what it meant, but he'd seen it written on rest-room walls, and he knew his mother would kill him if she heard him.

Somebody wanted to kill him. Didn't they? Or did they? How could he know for sure? What should he do?

Call the police, maybe. There was an extension phone in his mother's room, if the place wasn't full of people.

He heard them in the hall, a bunch of feminine voices, and then they were moving away toward the stairs. "Someone's got to be at the church and the reception hall," he heard Teddi say clearly, and then her voice was lost in the clamor of the others. All the girl cousins, running around, looking at the bridal gown and the bridesmaids' dresses and the blue, lacy garter and all the other junk.

That was all that was important. Darcy's wedding, and all the things that went with it. It didn't matter if someone shot Rob, or dropped a pot on his head and knocked him cold.

He opened the door and looked out. The last of them were vanishing down the stairs, giggling. He swallowed the painful lump in his throat and crossed the hall to where his parents' door stood open.

There were wedding signs here, too, in the tuxedo his father would wear, which was hanging from the top of the closet door, and his mother's long dress to go with it. The bridesmaid dress that had been altered for Ellen Anderson lay across the bed, its folds carefully arranged so as not to muss the skirt. But the room was empty.

Rob went in and closed the door behind him, shutting off the sounds from the lower part of the house.

The police number was there on a red sticker on the base of the phone, along with the fire department, the ambulance, and the doctor's phone numbers. He dialed it, willing his finger to stay steady.

"City Police," said a gruff voice.

Rob cleared his throat. "I want to report . . . that somebody's trying to kill me."

There was a brief silence. Then the voice, deeper than before, said, "Look, sonny, it's against the law to play jokes like that with the police department. You can get in trouble."

"I'm already in trouble." For a moment his eyes were so swimmy that the clothes hanging on the closet door shimmered and melted in front of him. "Please, I'm really in trouble."

"What's your name?" the officer asked.

"Robert Mallory."

"Do your folks know you're using the telephone?"

"No, I . . ." His throat ached so that it was hard to talk. "Nobody will listen to me. Look, somebody shot at me . . . at first I thought it was just some dumb kid shooting a .22 without paying attention where he shot, but then the pot fell out of the window almost on me . . ."

"How old are you, son?"

He didn't see what difference that made to anything, but he told the man, anyway. "Eleven."

"Have you been taking something? Some pills, something somebody gave you?"

"No!" Indignation rippled through him. "I'm not . . . not . . . it's true! Someone tried to kill me! Twice!"

"Did you get hold of something belongs to your mother, maybe? Something out of her purse, or out of the medicine cabinet?"

He was shaking so badly now that he had to use both hands to hold the phone. "No." He remembered to make his voice quiet, not yell. "No, I didn't take anything. I saw this . . . this murder, and now somebody wants to kill me before I can tell . . ."

"You like to watch television?" the man asked. "You like those horror shows?"

"I'm not making it up, I didn't get it from any television show! This old lady was killed, and I saw it, and now he wants to shut me up . . ."

"Who? Who is he, this man who wants to kill you?"

"I don't know, I only saw his hands, but he killed her, and he must know I saw him . . ."

"And he killed somebody?" There was no change in the voice, no indication that Rob was being taken seriously. "When was this?"

"This morning! This morning, right next door!"

"And he killed an old lady? Who was she?"

Was the man beginning to believe him? He'd have to believe him, wouldn't he, if he knew about Mrs. Calloway? Rob swallowed and firmed his voice. "Mrs. Calloway. Right next door."

"Calloway." The man on the other end of the line turned his head from the receiver, speaking to someone else in the same room with him. "Hey, Joe, what was the name of that old gal Riley and Fritz brought in this morning, the one got hanged with her binocular strap? Was it Calloway?"

107

The reply was quite loud; the other speaker must be very near the phone. "Yeah, that's right. Fell out a window and the strap caught on a tree branch. Freak accident."

"Upstairs window, was it?"

"Naw, first floor. They said her toes were only a foot or so off the ground. What's up?"

"Kid says he saw the old lady murdered. They send a crew out to investigate?"

"Yeah, they checked it out. Accident, pure and simple. The old woman fell out a window and caught that strap on the tree. Who'd try to murder anybody, pushing 'em out a window six feet off the ground?"

Slowly Rob replaced the receiver. It was no use. The police didn't believe him either. Maybe they were right. It seemed so crazy, maybe he'd just made it all up in his head.

There was a picture of his father on the dresser, on his mother's side of the big bed. It had been taken a long time ago, when his father had more hair and less midsection, but it looked pretty much the way he did now. Calm, smiling, reasonable.

Reasonable. His father was almost always reasonable. He'd be home pretty soon now, wouldn't he? And he'd listen. Rob would make him listen. He wouldn't yell or cry or do anything that turned people off, he'd just tell him the facts, and his father would listen, the way he always did.

A few hours wouldn't matter, would they? Whoever it was who'd shot at him, they couldn't get at him here, in his own house. So he'd be perfectly safe until his father came home.

10

The afternoon passed slowly. Nobody came near him, although he heard voices coming and going outside his door. He knew when Teddi and Max and Derek came back from delivering the champagne. Derek left again to get his car fixed, then came back much later. One of the girl cousins fell downstairs and had to be carried into Teddi's room, sobbing loudly. He heard her mother decide it was no more serious than a sprained ankle, and his mother offer the use of an Ace Bandage.

Rob listened to his radio and tried to fix the *Constitution,* but it was a project so hopeless that he soon abandoned it and threw the remains in the waste basket. It was warm in the room. He opened both windows and sat for a time staring at the house next door. There were the same old-fashioned lace curtains on the second floor as on the first, so that you couldn't see into any of the rooms. He wondered if there was still someone over there, watching from behind the heavy curtains.

So far as he knew, the police hadn't locked up the house. The window downstairs, the one she'd fallen out of, was hidden by the foliage of the cherry tree, but he knew it was still open. Probably there were other open windows, too, so that anybody could get in if he wanted to. Anybody at all.

In the movies there's always a motive for a murder. It wasn't hard to think of reasons why anybody would hate Mrs. Calloway. Everybody in town had some reason to *dislike* her.

Like old Max. She'd called the cops on him because he ran over her stupid hose. Of course the cops hadn't arrested him or anything like that, so it probably wasn't a very *strong* motive. Still, sometimes people were killed for little things, like sixty-seven cents.

Whoever was in there with her had been talking to her. She'd said crossly, "I will not," as if he'd asked her to do something. Maybe it was something he wanted really bad. Maybe, he thought with a flash of insight, it was something like his Uncle Ray. Maybe the man had done something . . . stolen something . . . and wanted her to forget about it (if it was from her) or help him, the way Uncle Ray had asked his father to do. And then she'd said, "You must be out of your mind to think I'd agree to any such thing."

If his request had been as bad as all that, maybe he'd been really desperate. Desperate enough to want to kill her.

But he couldn't have thought pushing her out that first floor window would kill her.

It all came back to that. His mind went around and around, in a circle.

Maybe he hadn't *meant* to kill her, but had pushed

her in anger, and then when she died he realized someone had seen him. Even if he didn't intend to murder her, he'd be guilty of *something*. If Rob told on him, he'd most likely go to jail or at least be disgraced when the story came out in the paper.

So he had to shut Rob up before he told anyone.

How could the man be sure it wasn't already too late? How could he be sure Rob hadn't already told everybody?

He grimaced, kicking at a chair with the toe of one tennis shoe. If he came around *this* house, he'd soon realize nobody was listening to anything today.

The telephone rang several times, but it was always answered downstairs. He couldn't tell who it was. If his father called to say he wasn't coming home . . . but he wouldn't do that, no matter what was happening to Uncle Ray. His father had to be at the wedding rehearsal at 7:30, or he wouldn't know what to do at the wedding tomorrow.

S.O.B. appeared suddenly in one of the open windows. He frequently came and went this way, over the roof, up and down the surrounding trees.

"Hi," Rob greeted him. "Does your tail hurt?"

The cat just looked superior, and then Rob saw why.

"Hey, you brought home a friend!"

The other cat almost stopped, putting one paw delicately on the windowsill, not stepping over it. S.O.B. leaped onto the other bed and began to wash himself.

"Hey, you're a beauty! Come on in," Rob invited softly.

The cat was a Siamese, as elegant as S.O.B. was tough.

111

"Come on," Rob coaxed. "Come on in, I won't hurt you."

He backed away and stood still, so as not to frighten her. S.O.B. uttered a throaty sort of growl (also an invitation?) and the Siamese gathered courage and entered the room. Light on her feet, oh, very light . . . a beautiful cat. A valuable one. Somebody would be looking for her.

It took a little time to get her to allow him to touch her. He had plenty of time. He stroked the silky fur and was pleased when she began to purr, not a loud rumble like S.O.B. but a refined, rolling murmur.

Someone tapped at the door.

Rob turned, waiting. "Come on in."

Nothing happened. After a moment he crossed the room and flung open the door.

There was no one in the hallway, but there was a tray on the floor. A tray, with a bottle of pop and something covered with a dish towel.

Well, they weren't going to starve him, then, even if he was an outcast. He picked up the tray, glad that his mother had relented at least this much. He knew her well enough to be sure that when she found out the true story she would be very sorry and very apologetic. Still, that didn't help a lot right now.

He carried the tray over to his desk and took off the covering towel. Somebody'd been to the delicatessen, obviously. There was fried chicken, and some of his mother's potato salad, and a couple of buttered rolls and some carrot sticks.

For once he didn't have an appetite; too much worry, he decided. But the pop was cold and he drank some of that and chewed on a carrot stick. The

Siamese and S.O.B. were watching him.

"It's not cat food," he informed them, but they kept right on watching until S.O.B. suddenly rose, stretching his muscles, and strolled to the window ledge. He gave Rob a nasty look and bounded out over the roof.

The Siamese remained where she was, eyeing the dinner tray.

"Are you really hungry?" Rob said. The cat emitted a plaintive sound, and he gave in. "Okay. Have a chicken leg. I don't need all the chicken anyway. Maybe I'll be sorry if I have to stay up here much longer, though, if this is all they bring me."

The cat ate daintily, stripping the meat off the bone, chewing with excellent manners, then washing her face.

"Kitty!"

Rob spun, lips tightening. Little Neddy stood in the doorway, one blond curl falling over his forehead. There was a purplish lump on his forehead, too, but Neddy wasn't fussing over that any more. He advanced into the room, arms extended toward the Siamese.

"That's *my* kitty."

"You better not touch it; it might scratch," Rob told him. "And if it does, that will be my fault too, I suppose."

"It's *my* kitty." Neddy looked at him with defiance, reaching for the cat. Rob made a move to stop him, but Neddy had already scooped up the creature in both arms, holding it dangling from the middle. "It's my kitty."

Seeing that the Siamese was evidently used to

children and wasn't going to cause any major injuries, Rob shrugged. "Okay. Go play somewhere else."

Contented, Neddy dragged the cat down the hall. Rob was still standing in the doorway watching him when the phone rang.

He heard Teddi's clear voice sing out from below, "Mom, it's Dad! He wants to talk to you!"

Rob tensed. He'd been expecting his father momentarily; did this mean there'd been another delay?

He moved out to the head of the stairs, straining to hear at least his mother's side of the conversation. He did, even over the low murmur of voices from the living room.

"Oh, Wally, no! Why? Well, how are we going to manage if you don't get back for the rehearsal? . . ."

Rob missed a few words, struggling with his own emotions. His father had to get home tonight, he had to!

"Well, I suppose so, but it seems to me that in a once-in-a-lifetime situation like this, the wedding should take precedence over anything else . . . why can't you tell me what it's all about?"

He had to talk to his father. Rob began to run down the hall, pushing open the door to his parents' room, snatching up the extension phone.

"Dad . . . Dad, please, I've got to talk to you . . ."

He'd kept on talking, even when he knew it was too late. The downstairs phone clicked off as soon as he picked it up; he heard his father hang up, too, out there wherever he was.

Rob blinked hard against the sting in his eyes. He should have run to the other phone the minute it

114

rang, he shouldn't have waited until he knew for sure his father wasn't coming home . . .

He hung up, defeated. What if his father didn't come home tonight at all? What was he going to do, stay hidden here in the house forever? They'd be going to the rehearsal pretty soon, the rest of them . . . the ones that mattered, anyway. There was no point in trying to make any of his out-of-town relatives understand his predicament. Ever since he'd got stuck in that sewer pipe years ago, they'd acted like he had two heads and neither of them worked. Nobody would listen to him, or help him.

His steps were slow, returning to his own room. He'd always liked the room and felt sort of lucky that he didn't have to share it with some creep of a brother, like Paddy's, who had a fit every time you dropped a sock on the floor. Only today it seemed like a prison.

He guessed his father was still trying to do something to keep Uncle Ray out of prison. For the first time he really thought about what it would be like, to be in jail. He wouldn't have a room like this one, either, with carpet on the floors and bright wallpaper and spreads and his own books and the tummy TV and radio-record player.

For a time he imagined that he was in a prison, behind bars, walking on cold concrete floors. Imagined what the food would be like, the clothes, the other prisoners. He even went back further and imagined what he'd done to get into prison in the first place; not borrowing some money he thought he could pay back, but maybe for armed robbery. That meant with a gun, threatening somebody.

Every once in a while there was a burst of laughter from downstairs, as if everyone else was having a heck of a good time. And under his windows, on the side lawn, the girl cousins were playing some silly game and giggling and giggling. He was glad he didn't have any sisters that age.

After a time the game of imagining himself in jail grew boring. He sat in front of one of the windows, welcoming the slight breeze, watching what he could see of the activity below.

The grown-ups had moved outside now, probably because it was getting cooler, and little Neddy was there with the Siamese cat, dragging it around by its neck. Nobody seemed to be paying any attention until Max's voice suddenly rose over the general hum of conversation.

"Hey, what's the matter with that cat?"

Rob leaned forward to see better, but they were out of his line of vision. The girl cousins had stopped playing, though, and were looking toward the house. They weren't laughing anymore. One of them had her mouth open.

"Good grief, is it having some kind of fit?" Mrs. Mallory demanded. "Where did it come from, anyway? Is it your cat, Sylvester?"

"Never saw it 'til Neddy came dragging it downstairs. You know what it looks like, Marge, it's got poisoned or something. You got rat poison out, or ant poison, or anything like that?"

As the other voices hushed, Rob could hear clearly what was being said. He hung as far out over the sill as he dared, but he still couldn't see anything except

116

a bunch of heads as the people gathered around the cat.

"I seen a dog like that once, in convulsions, sort of. They took it to the vet and saved its life. Something ought to be done with it, or it's going to die."

"Derek? Max?" Mrs. Mallory asked, sounding uncertain.

"I'm allergic to cats," Derek said, but Max spoke at the same time. "Sure, I'll go, if somebody can hold the cat. Get a towel or something to wrap it in, so you don't get scratched."

"Maybe it's got rabies," someone suggested.

"Naw, it's poisoned," Sylvester insisted. "I seen the dog, did the same thing, like that. You better hurry, or there's no use going at all."

Rob felt as if something had caught his heart and lungs in a giant vise, squeezing so that he couldn't breathe, yet the blood was throbbing in his ears so loud he could hear it.

Poisoned. The cat had been poisoned.

He didn't think Neddy had let go of it since he'd carried it out of Rob's room, so it hadn't had time to get into anything like ant poison, even if there was any around. He didn't think there was, or somebody would have told him.

But just before Neddy took the cat downstairs, it had had something to eat. A bit of the chicken off Rob's tray.

He licked his lips, staring at the tray, and he thought he was going to be sick. Whoever the murderer was, he was right there in the house.

11

He hadn't eaten any of the chicken, simply because he wasn't hungry. He lost what he had eaten, and it left him shaky and weak-feeling. He stared at his reflection in the bathroom mirror. Boy, Darcy'd really have cause for complaint if his pictures came out looking like he did right now. His skin had a greenish cast, and the black eye was grotesque along with it. There were Frankensteinlike scabs healing over the scratches. He could play a part in a horror movie without any makeup, just the way he was.

It could be he was jumping to conclusions. His father sometimes chided his mother with the words, "Honey, you're jumping to conclusions. You don't have enough evidence to know that for sure."

He rinsed out his mouth and spat in the sink, making his way slowly back down the hall. He didn't have any real evidence, either. Maybe the cat ate something just before he came in the window with S.O.B., something that was poisoned. Rob didn't have any idea how long it took poison to work. Some kinds he thought were pretty fast, other kinds took a longer time.

The cat was hungry when it came in. Really hungry, Rob remembered. He didn't think it had had anything to eat since it got lost. Which would mean the only thing that could have poisoned it was the chicken.

His first impulse was to destroy the remaining chicken, before anything else could happen. He actually picked up the tray before he realized how foolish that would be. If there was one thing he needed, it was to have some concrete evidence that he wasn't making this all up. Poisoned food would have to convince them all.

Where to put it, then? Maybe whoever it was would expect him to eat it all, so there wouldn't be anything left to test. But if he didn't die, it would be clear he hadn't eaten it, right? And so whoever it was would look for it, because if the person had been seen bringing up the tray he wouldn't want any proof around that it had poisoned food on it.

He'd look in Rob's room for it, if he got the chance. So this wasn't a good place to keep it.

Darcy's room, he decided. She'd be there yet tonight, but she wouldn't be poking around in odd corners. Her luggage was all packed for her honeymoon; the stuff she was wearing to get married in was all right out in plain sight because she'd been showing it to everybody.

He didn't know if the poison was on everything, or just the chicken. He looked it over carefully, but he couldn't see anything different about it. He'd eaten a little of the potato salad and some carrot sticks, so he guessed they'd been all right. He hoped they had. He hoped it wasn't just taking longer to work because he was bigger than the cat.

Everybody was downstairs. They'd all had something to eat and pretty soon they'd be leaving for the church, the ones who were in the wedding party, for the rehearsal. He didn't know if they'd have to come back upstairs for anything before they went or not, but he'd better hurry, just in case.

Darcy's room was a mess. He stared around it, wondering why his mother had such a fit about his room when Darcy's was so much worse.

Her bridal finery was hung all over, and there were open suitcases on the bed and two chairs, and he could see six pairs of shoes on the floor without even walking all the way into the room. She'd packed a few things to take to the new apartment, and the open boxes stood about.

Where should he hide the poisoned chicken? He wondered, if nobody found it for a while, if the food itself spoiled, would they still be able to detect the poison?

He thought so. He remembered a TV movie where they'd dug up this guy's remains after he'd been buried for months, and they'd been able to tell that he'd been murdered by a poisoner.

So if he put it where a searcher wouldn't expect it to be, and where somebody'd be sure to find it sooner or later, even if something happened to Rob himself so he couldn't point it out to them, they'd know, wouldn't they?

He bent over one of the cartons destined for Darcy's apartment. This one looked likely; it contained shampoo, bath oil, powder, and junk like that. She'd dig into the box as soon as she got home. He lifted out the top layer of bottles and boxes and tucked in the remaining pieces of chicken carefully wrapped in the dish towel. Then he replaced the items, noting that it looked no different from before.

All right, what was he going to do now?

Think, first. Think about who had brought up the tray.

Not a peace offering from his mother. That he was sure of. Although she might have suggested that he be fed, she hadn't been the one to carry it upstairs.

He realized now that it should have seemed odd to him when whoever it was knocked on the door, put the tray on the floor, and then went away. *He didn't want to be seen.*

Of course he must have carried the tray through the house, and it was filled with people milling around. But there were far too many to eat at the dining room table, where he knew his mother had set out a buffet supper. They'd carried their trays and paper plates all over the place, including out into the yard and onto the porches. So nobody would think twice about one more person carrying some food around.

A man. It was a man he'd seen. But there weren't many men it could have been.

A man who had free access to the Mallory house. Mrs. Calloway had died long before his relatives had arrived, and they didn't know her, anyway. Walt Mallory was gone . . . not that his father was a suspect, he'd been right here in the house when Rob came tearing in to report the old lady's death, and while he might get really mad at her, he wouldn't have pushed her out a window.

121

Steve had gone off somewhere for Darcy. So he couldn't have brought the tray up. Max was down there, or had been until he went tearing off to the vet's with the cat. And Derek. Derek had said he was allergic to cats, although he'd never mentioned it before now.

Max and Derek. Was that all the possibilities? Was it Max or Derek?

It didn't seem possible it could be either one. He'd known them both all his life. They started coming around when Darcy went to high school, years ago. They took her to movies and dances and ball games, and they raided the Mallory refrigerator the same as the family did. Max had a job installing furnaces, and Derek had a big scholarship to learn to be something important, Rob forgot what. Ordinary, everyday guys.

Max? Or Derek?

They both had reason to dislike the old lady, maybe even to hate her. But it took a pretty strong motive, usually, to kill somebody.

Like, to get their money, or keep them from telling something about you that would make you go to jail, or something like that. Old Lady Calloway didn't have any money that Rob knew of. She griped about every penny she had to spend on anything, like that crummy old hose she'd put in the street so Max would have to run over it.

Fifteen dollars for a hose was high, Max said, but he wouldn't have killed her to keep from buying a hose, would he?

And Derek? He was Mrs. Calloway's nephew. He didn't usually fight with her, because he didn't see any more of her than he had to. He seldom went into the house. He'd told Rob once that it stunk.

Only the two of them for suspects?

He thought about it and decided it *had* to be one of them. Max or Derek. Derek or Max.

He was feeling very strange. Sort of clammy, as if he were sweating, although it wasn't nearly so hot now. And like his stomach was really empty, but the thought of food made him afraid he'd throw up again.

Max and Derek had been friends of the family since they were all kids. How could one of them be a murderer? How could one of them seriously try to kill Rob?

And then he remembered.

There was a way to tell which of them it was.

S.O.B. had scratched at the outstretched arms. The murderer would carry the marks of the cat's powerful claws.

He tried to remember what each of them had been wearing earlier in the day. It took a little real thought, because he didn't usually notice people's ordinary clothes.

Max . . . Max was wearing white western jeans and a blue shirt. The shirt had long sleeves.

And Derek was wearing . . . brown slacks and a yellow shirt. Also with long sleeves.

He heard them coming back, heard their voices, Max's and Teddi's, although they were too close to the house to be visible.

"Did you get there on time?"

"Is the cat still alive?"

"Was it poisoned?"

123

Rob strained to catch Max's report. "She was poisoned; they're not sure with what. Maybe somebody put bait out for squirrels or something; they thought it was strychnine, although it's illegal to use it."

"Did she die?"

"No, they gave her a shot of something that knocked her out. Doc Hansen said there's a good chance she'll pull through."

"He recognized the cat, too." That was Teddi, sounding pleased. "It belongs to some people named Ellsworth, about three blocks from here. The cat's been missing since yesterday. I don't know how it got into our house."

"Probably that big ugly thing of yours got himself a girl friend," Sylvester suggested, and Rob heard the ripple of laughter.

Rob's mouth was dry. Would they believe him, if he went down right now and told them he'd fed the cat some of his chicken? Would they take the remaining pieces wherever you had to take it to find out if it was poisoned?

Or would they continue to be annoyed with him, accuse him of making it up, being dramatic, trying to steal the limelight from Darcy's wedding?

If they didn't believe him, he'd be in worse shape than he was in now, wouldn't he? Because whichever of them it was didn't want him to convince anyone of what he'd seen from the cherry tree, he was down there, right now, mingling with the others.

"Now what?" There was a different note in Uncle Sylvester's words. He had a deep, booming voice that carried over all the others. "Police car stopping in front, Marge. I swear, this is the jumpin'est place I ever saw."

"I can't imagine . . ." That was his mother, sounding worried. "It can't be Wally . . . I talked to him just a few . . ."

Rob couldn't see the front of the house from where he was. He slipped quickly down the hall to look out the windows at the top of the stairs.

Sure enough, there was the same police car as had come when Old Lady Calloway died. Riley and Fritz. They sure worked long hours.

Cripes, had they come here to arrest him for making that blamed phone call?

Stupid. Everything he did was stupid. He shouldn't have said his name until the officer sounded like he believed it wasn't some dumb kid trick.

Rob's pulse speeded up and he felt as if he were smothering. He couldn't hear anything they said to his mother and his uncle, who had walked to the front curb, because the window was closed. If he opened it, they'd hear him; it would only draw attention to himself.

He wished desperately he could make out their words. They didn't even stand facing him, so there wasn't any chance of guessing by watching their lips. Fritz threw out a hand toward Mrs. Calloway's house, and then he saw his mother turn and look up at him.

She couldn't see him. He knew that, because he was looking through the curtains. But he felt as if she could. She looked . . . what? Upset? Angry?

He stood there, watching, as long as they talked.

125

And then they started, all four of them, toward the house.

They were coming to get him. Rob waited no longer. He fled.

12

There wasn't time to stop and get anything to take with him, not a sweater for if it got cold or the Mounds bar he had hidden in his desk drawer for an emergency, or anything at all.

They'd be coming up the front stairs, and he had to be out of sight by the time they got to the top.

He didn't make the mistake of getting trapped in his own room; there was no escape from that, not unless you were a surefooted cat who could stroll along the slanting shingles of the roof.

No, the only way out, except down the stairs, was through the window that stood open for ventilation at the back end of the hall. There was a drop of some six or eight feet to the roof over the utility room. Rob slipped over the sill and jumped, rolling a little on the sloping surface, thinking for sure he'd go over the edge and break his back on the walk below.

He didn't, though. His hands found the small pipe that came up from the drains in the back bathroom. It slowed him down and he dropped to the ground only seconds before he heard his mother's voice.

"Robbie! Where are you?"

It was nowhere near dark yet. If anybody was around, they'd see him, sure.

It seemed that no one was, though; they'd all been drawn toward the police car and hadn't yet filtered back into the rear yard.

Where was he going to go?

He didn't know. The only thing he was sure of was that he had to stay out of sight, out of everybody's sight, until his father got home. He had complete faith in him; his father wouldn't let them put him in jail, or lock him in his room, or make any more attempts on his life. Rob was certain of that.

But until his father came home, he had to disappear. He wasn't safe even in his own house; if the police didn't arrest him, he'd still be fair game for a killer.

It was S.O.B. who gave him the idea.

Rob moved cautiously along the rear wall of the house, peering to see if any of the giggling little girls still wandered about between the houses. They were all gone, except one he especially disliked. Her name was Annabel, and she was about his own age. Once when he'd visited her family, she had hit him in the head with a rock and he'd had to have three stitches.

Annabel was sneaking up on S.O.B., asleep on the porch steps. Rob wanted to shout a warning, but this was one time S.O.B. would have to take his chances. Not that he couldn't handle Annabel, as far as that went.

The girl pounced, scooping the animal up against her plump chest. S.O.B., outraged, squalled a protest and wrenched himself free, leaving a long red streak down Annabel's arm.

"Rotten old cat, anyway," she said after him, as S.O.B. streaked toward the cherry tree. He was up the tree and through the open window into Mrs. Calloway's house before she could chase him.

The girl stood for a moment, looking at her scratched arm, muttering. Then she gave an angry kick at something lying in the grass beside the steps, sending it rolling almost to Rob's feet, and went into the house, slamming the door behind her.

His jar of spiders. Rob stooped to pick it up, noting that the lid was about to come off. That stupid Annabel, she'd have let them all go, after he'd spent hours collecting them. If he left it sitting around in the yard they'd be gone, for sure. If Neddy found them and got the lid off and they found him with spiders crawling all over him, Rob knew there'd be some fits then, all right.

It was really too large a jar to fit into his pocket; he heard the seam rip when he forced it in, and it made an awkward bulge in his pants, but it was either that or abandon the spiders.

Rob hesitated, for there was no way of telling whether or not anyone was looking out the windows on this side of the house. They were all tattletales. Anybody who saw him would tell his mother, and the police. He knew that from past experience. But he had to take the chance.

S.O.B. was now inside the deserted house. Rob dashed for the cherry tree, flinging himself up into its familiar welcoming branches. Not that he was safe there for long; too many people knew how much time he spent in the tree. He wondered if the garage across the alley was unlocked; sometimes it was. Only he'd have to spend too long in the open getting to it. Any minute they'd come out, looking for him, the police . . . and maybe the murderer . . . all of them.

He stared at the opening through which the cat had disappeared. There was no reason to be afraid of the house any longer; Mrs. Calloway was gone. He couldn't see S.O.B. in there, but he was prowling around somewhere, so it wouldn't be quite like being in there alone.

An idea struck him so sharply that he held his breath for a few seconds. Was there any chance the killer had left clues inside the house? In all the movies, the murderer returns to the scene of the crime to destroy the evidence.

The blood seemed to move thickly in his ears; the idea both frightened and excited him. Maybe if he found some evidence, and then hid and watched it . . . maybe one of them would come, to see about it.

The screen door slammed behind him. He didn't wait to see who it was; it didn't matter, because any of them would give him away. Rob breathed deeply and took the same path as the cat, out along the thick branch that stretched to the open window.

At the moment he was over the end of it that had held Mrs. Calloway's dangling body he felt a reluctance to go any further, but the sound of voices behind him was a spur. He swallowed and moved the rest of the way along the limb, reaching out with a foot for the windowsill, easing himself through the opening.

For some time he didn't go any further, didn't even look around. Safe behind the lace curtains, he could look out across the grassy expanse between the two houses. The tree itself cut off some of the view, but it didn't keep the voices from reaching him.

"Robbie! Robbie, where are you?" That was his mother. She sounded upset.

"Does he have friends nearby where he could go, Mrs. Mallory?" That was the cop, Riley. "It might be smart to check with his friends, if you could tell us who they are. Make up a list, maybe."

"Yes, of course, if you think that'll help. Although I can't imagine . . . this isn't like Rob, at all."

Darcy's clear tone carried from the porch. "What shall we do, Mom? The rehearsal's set for twenty minutes from now. Shall I call and say we can't make it? I don't know if we can even notify everybody in that length of time . . . some of them have probably already started for the church."

Mrs. Mallory's hesitation was brief. "No. Go on and go. It doesn't matter whether I'm there or not. All I have to do is walk down the aisle on the arm of the usher, isn't it? We'll have to brief your father later, anyway, when he gets here. The rest of you might as well go ahead as planned."

Steve, back now, sounded uncertain for the first time since Rob had known him. "Do you think . . . should we postpone the wedding, Mrs. Mallory?"

"With 250 people coming?" She sounded as if she were strangling, Rob thought. "No, of course not. This is going to be straightened out, Rob's just . . . just wandered off somewhere, he'll turn up. Go on."

The voices blended, blurred, the words impossible to catch as people moved toward the cars in front or back into the house. Rob hadn't seen her approach, so he jumped when Teddi spoke from only a few feet away.

"Robbie? Robbie, it's me, Teddi. Do you hear me? Answer me, Robbie! I won't let anyone hurt you, don't you know that?"

By shifting position slightly, he could see her. She was looking up into the cherry tree, her head thrown back, concern written on her familiar features.

How could she promise anything, when the police were right there, ready to take him into custody? Even so, the urge to say something was overwhelming. Teddi he trusted. If he told her not to tell where he was, she wouldn't.

He actually parted his lips, ready to speak her name, when he saw that Max was with her. Old Max, also looking anxious. Old Max, with his long-sleeved blue shirt that might conceal the marks of S.O.B.'s claws.

Rob squinted, trying to see Max's hands and at the same time to remember again the hands that had pushed the old woman. He wasn't successful either way; Max had his hands in his pockets and all he could remember about the murderer's hands was that they were large.

"He isn't in the tree, Teddi. He usually sits right there, in that crotch. It's the only comfortable place to sit. Besides, he wouldn't he hiding in the cherry tree; he knows we all know he goes up there."

Rob bit his lower lip. If it were only Teddi, he would take a chance. With Max there, he didn't dare. Not if there was a possibility that Max was the one who was after him.

Teddi turned away; there was a tremor in her voice. "If I could just talk to him . . . he must be horribly upset."

"He'll turn up," Max assured her. "Come on, you've got to practice being a bridesmaid. We'd better get going with the rest of them."

"You're coming along?"

"Sure. You need a ride over and back, don't you? I'll leave you off and come back in an hour, right? Afterward maybe we can . . ."

"Afterward we're coming back here." Teddi's tone had firmed. "Until I'm sure Robbie's all right."

"Of course he's all right, but we'll come back. Whatever you want. Let's go."

Rob, watching through the heavy lace, felt a little bit the way the captain must feel, left on his sinking ship as the last of his crew is transferred to another vessel. He had to kneel at the window in order to get any sort of view; he leaned against the sill, welcoming the steadying influence of something immovable, until he realized that he was causing the curtains to pull tight. That would give him away, if anyone looked at them.

Car doors slammed, voices mingled unintelligibly. When the wedding party was gone, there were still plenty of people around. Including the police, whom he could see still talking to his mother, although he couldn't make out their words. Not until they left, when Fritz called out, "Well, you give us a call when he turns up, Mrs. Mallory. We'll be in touch later, anyway, just in case."

Just in case what? Rob wondered. He got a glimpse

of his mother's face as she turned toward the house; she looked very tired and almost as if she were about to cry.

"Why don't you let me fix you a drink, Marge? You sure look like you need one," Sylvester suggested, touching her arm.

"What I need," Mrs. Mallory said, her voice wavering, "is for Wally to come home. Or even call. I'd settle for a call right now."

"Well, sure, that will make you feel better, when he comes. But there's nothing he can do that the rest of us can't . . . we'll get the kids out looking around the neighborhood, and the police are going to check with all his buddies. In the meantime, anything that'll help hold you together ought to be to the good, hadn't it? Let's all have a martini, just to put things in perspective."

They went inside and for a time Rob crouched where he was, until there was no one outside except the girl cousins and Neddy, who had somehow appropriated an orange-colored stuffed lion that belonged to Teddi. He felt a surge of resentment on Teddi's behalf; he knew darned well she hadn't said the little brat could play with the lion. She kept it on the foot of her bed, and she wouldn't want it to get dirty.

Behind him Rob heard small sounds that brought him about with neck-cracking speed, his eyes wide.

He'd never been inside this house before, had had only a glimpse of it through the window. It was heavily, ornately furnished with very old things, sort of like his grandmother had, only his grandmother's house smelled of cookies and baking bread and lemon furniture polish. This place smelled of old sweat and musty carpeting and strange unpleasant things he couldn't identify.

The sounds were S.O.B., probing the goldfish bowl with one sturdy paw. There was a flash of color, and the orangy fish slithered down the cat's throat. S.O.B. eyed Rob with ears back, twitching, expectant.

There was only one fish left in the bowl.

Rob exhaled slowly. "Go ahead, who cares? Nobody else wants them, anyway."

S.O.B. continued to watch him, yellow eyes glittering.

"You just startled me. That's why I jumped. You don't think I'm afraid of being in here, do you? Just because it's *her* house? She's dead and carried away, and there's nothing here to hurt anybody. It's just an empty house."

He hoped the cat didn't notice that his words were slightly unsteady. Because it was true, of course, that there was nothing to be afraid of in the empty house. Nobody knew he was here.

He got up, then, and looked around. There were plants all over the place, green things with all kinds of leaves, growing in pots. Most of them didn't have any flowers. He wondered why she liked just all those leaves, with nothing on them. They were kind of creepy.

That reminded him of the pot that had been dropped on him from the second floor. Maybe if he went up there he'd find a clue of some kind.

He had no idea where the stairs were. He'd have to

135

poke around and find them. Although it was still broad daylight outside, it was rather murky in here because of the heavy curtains, and a lot of the shades were down. Mrs. Calloway must have been part mole.

For a split second he remembered her as he had seen her this morning, the leather strap twisted around her neck, her mouth open, her blue eyes bulging. He put the memory aside quickly. She was dead, and he didn't believe in ghosts.

Still, he was glad to have S.O.B.'s company as he moved through the lower rooms.

Mrs. Calloway hadn't been a very good housekeeper. There was dust on everything, and the smell of mildew, and always that overpowering odor that seemed a combination of medicine and unwashed bodies and rotting garbage.

Rob moved slowly, opening doors slowly, especially in the darker rooms. On the threshold of one room he stopped, his throat closing on a yell he couldn't make, for there was a figure in the middle of the floor.

Once more he exhaled slowly, allowing his heartbeat to slow. Only one of those dressmaker dummy things. The room was a clutter of ancient treadle sewing machine, bags and boxes of materials and buttons, and newspapers. Cripes, there must be ten years' worth of newspapers stacked up in the corners.

He moved into the tower room. From it he had a view up and down the street, both ways, and of all the houses on the other side of the road. He could well believe she hadn't missed much from here, even if she hadn't used the binoculars.

He came at last to the stairs. They weren't carpeted, like the ones at home, and they creaked beneath his weight. There was so much dust on the handrail that he couldn't think anyone had used it in years.

Yet someone had gone up there recently, someone had dropped the flowerpot in an attempt to hit him. Someone had shot at him.

There was a different aura about the second floor. At first he didn't know what it was, then he realized that the smell was no longer overpowering. It was musty and dusty, but the more unpleasant odors were all downstairs.

The room in which he was interested would be on the east side, toward the front, but not all the way. It ought to be that door, over there.

Rob stopped, unable to control the hammering in his chest. What if there were someone in there, the man who had shot at him . . .

It was silly, of course. The man hadn't stayed here. He'd gone downstairs and across the lawn and joined the wedding guests next door, waiting another chance at the boy who'd been unlucky enough to be watching when Mrs. Calloway was pushed out the window.

S.O.B. strolled past him, unalarmed, stirring up the dust of years. Rob moved, more slowly now, and gave the door a tentative push.

It was a big room, empty of furniture, the floor showing where the rug had been taken up from its center, and spots in the faded floral wallpaper showed where pictures had once been.

The only things still there were the curtains of heavy lace. Rob made his way toward the window, wondering if S.O.B. shared his tension, for the cat had turned and was looking at him in an oddly alert way.

Rob didn't have to move the curtains aside to see

that a man in this window would have a clear shot at anyone sitting on the Mallory steps.

There were scuff marks in the dust where the man had knelt; and further evidence—the first real proof he could present to the police and his parents that he wasn't making things up—there were three spent .22 shells. In this room where nobody had lived for more than a quarter of a century!

His first impulse was to scoop them up to show his father, but he remembered in time that the police liked to collect their own evidence. They might not believe him, that he'd found the shells here. On the other hand, there was the possibility that the shooter might remember the shells and come back for them, and who would then take Rob's word for their existence?

He ended by picking up one of them and slipping it into his pocket, leaving the other two untouched. If there had previously been any doubts in his own mind, they were now gone. This was no wild imagining, no jumping to conclusions. It was true. Someone had tried to kill him. And that someone would try again, if he could, until he succeeded.

"Dad will come home pretty soon," Rob said aloud, quietly. "When he does, I'll be all right."

He had no interest in further exploration of the house. It was too big, too gloomy, too dark in the corners. If the guilty man came back to destroy the evidence, it was to this room he would come. There was no need to watch any of the rest of the house.

He'd always thought of Mrs. Calloway as a witch, an evil storybook sort of person. Here in her house, he began to see her as a human being. There was a bag of knitting beside a chair in her sitting room. Some mending on a low table. A Bible open beside it, a faded purple ribbon marking the place.

Mrs. Calloway reading the Bible? It seemed unlikely, yet when he stared down at the pages he could see that she'd underlined various passages, the same way his grandmother did in her Bible.

Foxes have holes, and the birds of the air have nests; but the Son of Man hath nowhere to lay his head, he read.

Bleakly, Rob turned away. *I know how he must have felt.*

He wandered through into the kitchen, and then wished he hadn't. He'd never been in an untidier room. There were dirty dishes in the sink . . . not just today's dishes, but stacks of them. The stench of garbage was overpowering. A wide trail of ants led along a counter to where some sugar had been spilled; they were carrying it, grain by grain, down the wall and into a crack in the floor.

There were the remains of breakfast on the table, egg drying on a plate, coffee staining the painted wooden surface. And there were newspapers. Hundreds of them, everywhere. On the chairs, on top of the refrigerator, in heaps on the floor. She must have saved every paper she got in the past twenty years.

The floor hadn't been swept in days. He avoided what looked like a finger bone (for the witch from Hansel and Gretel?) and began to retreat toward the less filthy part of the house.

It was twilight, now, at least inside the house. They

ought to be coming back from the rehearsal pretty soon, and his father would surely be coming before long. All he had to do was stick it out until then, and he'd be all right.

He had reached the threshold of the dining room when he heard the footsteps on the back porch. The boards creaked under a man's weight.

Rob froze, unable to complete his step into the other room, unable to think fast enough to hide. Paralysis held him there, breathing painfully suspended, as the door began to open.

13

It was Derek, still wearing his brown slacks and yellow shirt. He hesitated as his eyes adjusted to the dimness.

He seemed somewhat disconcerted at seeing Rob. "Well, there you are. I ought to have guessed you'd hide over here." His hand groped for the wall switch, turning on a forty-watt bulb.

Rob couldn't have said anything if he'd tried.

Derek didn't seem to notice. "Boy, it sure stinks in here, doesn't it? Somebody'll have to come in and clean up the place."

S.O.B. came through the doorway, brushing Rob's ankles. He saw Derek and meowed plaintively.

"You hungry? Missed your supper, didn't you? How about you, Rob? You had anything to eat?"

Rob swallowed, but that was all. If he decided to run, where could he run to? The window in the dining room was open but he couldn't get through it in a hurry, probably not before Derek could catch up with him.

Was it Derek he had to fear? *Was it?*

"What are you hiding from?" Derek asked.

Was there malice in Derek's gaze, or was it only that the light from the small naked bulb cast his face into unaccustomed planes and shadows that made it seem so?

"For gosh sakes, Rob, you've got everybody thinking you're some kind of nut. Knocking babies around, calling the police with wild stories . . ." Derek's expression altered when he smiled. "What did you tell them that brought them roaring out here to talk to you?"

It was painful to swallow, but he kept having to do it or he couldn't seem to breathe. Rob forced his vocal cords to respond to his command.

"What did *they* say?"

"I didn't hear all of it. Just that you'd made some kind of phone call, and they were checking it out. Your mother's real upset with you. So's Darcy. Poor Darcy, she doesn't want her wedding spoiled."

"I haven't spoiled her wedding."

"Not yet," Derek agreed. "You told me something kind of far out, earlier . . . about Aunt Bea being pushed out the window. Was that what you told the police?"

Rob didn't answer.

"Was it true, then? I mean, you're not just having a field day taking off on stuff you got from TV; you really saw something this morning? What did you see?"

"Just what I told you. Somebody pushed her. I saw his hands. That's all. Just his hands."

"And you told that to the police?"

How dangerous was it to admit what he had said, if

Derek was the one who was stalking him? Dangerous, indeed, to admit to a killer that you hadn't been able to pass along to anyone else the evidence that would incriminate him.

"I don't remember what all I told them. They didn't seem to think I was serious, anyway."

"Was that why you ran away? Because of the police? But why, if you just wanted to tell them something that was true?"

"I didn't have any proof, then. Now I've got it."

Derek's features seemed to sharpen as he moved his head under the dangling light bulb. "You have? Proof of what? Proof against who?"

"I hid it . . . the evidence. Where they'll find it . . ." He almost said, "When Darcy comes back from her honeymoon," but that would provide a clue to where it was.

"What evidence did you find? What kind of clues does a man leave behind when he pushes someone out a window?"

Was he worried about it? Rob couldn't tell. There was the sound of a car outside and for a moment he hoped that it was his father. He'd run to the window and yell and Derek couldn't stop him and wouldn't dare do anything once his father had heard him. But the car didn't slow; it went on past, and there was a bitter, acrid taste in Rob's mouth.

"What evidence?" Derek insisted, stepping closer.

Rob wanted to retreat, but his back was against the doorframe.

"Why should I tell you? I'll tell my dad when he comes."

It was a touch of bravado not backed up by his ham-

143

mering heart. Derek didn't take offense. In fact, he grinned a little. "Why did you run when the police came?"

"They didn't believe me, before. They will when they see the evidence."

"But you're not going to tell me what it is?"

"No."

Derek shrugged, suddenly backing away. "Whew, the smell in here is unbelievable. Maybe if I just got rid of that garbage sack . . ."

He left the door standing open while he hauled out three bags of it, to dump into the can out back. He seemed to be inspecting it, shaking everything out of each bag as if it might contain something of value. He didn't leave the porch, and at no time was there any way Rob could have gone past him to escape.

"There, that's some better, isn't it? Why do you suppose she kept all the newspapers?" It didn't seem to bother him that Rob didn't reply. "Real fire hazard. Look at the way she's got them right next to the water heater. That's a gas heater, with a pilot light, and when the burner comes on . . . boy, the flame could shoot out and ignite those papers. This old place would go up like you wouldn't believe . . . I'll bet it would burn to the ground before they could even get the fire trucks here."

Rob felt the goose bumps rise on his bare arms at the implied threat. Or was it? Was Derek just talking?

"The evidence isn't here," Rob said. "It's . . . hidden. But where they'll find it, in a day or two."

Derek's grin seemed friendly, the same as always. "Yeah? Why don't you tell me what it is, Robbie?

Maybe I could help you . . . convincing the rest of them." He spoke casually, opening cupboard doors, peering into a paper bag, replacing it.

Rob stiffened against the use of his name. Nobody but his mother and grandmother called him Robbie anymore, except Teddi, once in a while when she forgot. "I don't need any help."

He did, though. Even if they found the poisoned chicken, would they know what to do with it? Would it occur to anybody that it ought to be tested for poison? If he weren't around to explain, it might not count for anything at all. The .22 shell would, if he could deliver it to someone who would listen . . . but if Derek burned the house down the other shells . . . and their location . . . would be lost forever.

I have to be around to tell people the connections, he thought. *And he knows it.*

Still, he couldn't be absolutely sure about Derek. His eyes drifted to the long sleeves of the yellow shirt. He'd know for sure if he saw Derek's arms. When S.O.B. scratched, he did a good job of it. There would be marks.

Rob blinked, realizing that Derek was watching him very closely and that he was no longer smiling.

"What's the matter, Robbie?"

"I think I'll go home," Rob said. "I'm getting hungry."

Derek glanced around the dimly lit kitchen. "Yeah? Well, there's food here, if you want a snack. *She* won't be needing it."

"I don't want any of her food."

Derek nodded. "I guess I don't blame you. She

145

wasn't very particular, was she? That's why my mother wouldn't come over here. Couldn't stand the smell and the mess. Poor Aunt Bea . . . she's probably better off dead. She was getting senile, and she didn't have much of a life."

Rob made a tentative move toward the back door. "I'll eat at home."

He wasn't sure whether Derek blocked his way by design or just happened to step in the same direction. At any rate, he occupied the space Rob would have to go through to get out.

"Don't you agree? She really isn't any great loss."

Maybe she wasn't, Rob thought, but that wasn't the point, was it? The police wouldn't think so.

Rob tried to reach past Derek for the doorknob, only to find the way barred by one muscular arm.

He was no match for Derek, physically; he knew that. Yet the suspense was more than he could bear, and he had to know the truth. Before Derek had any inkling of his intentions, Rob grabbed one yellow sleeve and ripped it upward. He used all his strength, and the button on the cuff popped off and rolled across the linoleum-covered floor.

Neither of them was aware of the button, however. They were looking at the exposed forearm, at the parallel red scratches made by a cat's claws.

Rob felt as if he couldn't breathe, and the need to swallow was uncontrollable. Derek's face was close, too close, above him.

His eyes had gone cold and peculiar in a way Rob couldn't have described, but instinct told him it was threatening. Derek's jaw showed dark, needing a shave, as it jutted dangerously.

146

"You shouldn't have done that, Robbie." The words were no more than a whisper, but that was all that was necessary to reach him, only inches away. "You shouldn't have done it."

It had been a calculated risk, and he had lost. If there had not been scratches, he might have found an ally; as it was, he had given away his own knowledge of the identity of a killer. And the killer knew he had not yet passed along any information to the authorities.

Very slowly, Derek pulled down his sleeve, his eyes still on Rob's waiting face. "I think there are some things you're going to tell me, Robbie."

He had never been more scared in his life, but he said the words that came, without thought, to his tongue. "Kiss off."

Slowly Derek reached for him, and took the one necessary step in his direction. As his fingers began to close around Rob's upper arm, his heel came down . . . on S.O.B.'s already injured tail.

The cat yowled and jumped; Derek staggered and loosened his hold, trying to regain his balance.

"That blasted cat! I'll kill it, too, you little bastard!"

S.O.B. streaked through the unlighted part of the house, disappearing into what was now almost full darkness.

As for Rob, the moment Derek's fingers let go, he stumbled backward, managed to turn, and fled. Through the dining room, snatching at the only thing he saw, the fishbowl that reflected the light from the kitchen. He flung it behind him, into the path of the pursuing Derek, and heard the muffled oath as it caught him in the shins.

Derek was too close to allow him to go through the window. Rob pounded on toward the front of the house, flinging himself at the front door, only to find it locked.

14

Although only a few seconds had passed it seemed to
Rob that he had been running for hours. This exit was
blocked to him; he glanced back to see Derek picking
himself up, kicking at the offending fishbowl.

The man was silhouetted against the lighted doorway into the kitchen, and clearly visible. Rob himself must be considerably harder to see, but there was
nowhere to go that he couldn't be heard.

He took the stairs. There was no logic to it, because
the upper floor was just as much a trap as where he
was . . . more, perhaps, because he couldn't drop
from one of those windows. But it would delay being
cornered, to go up there, whereas if he entered any of
these rooms, that would be the end. Right now, in
seconds.

His sneaker-clad feet pounded on the stairs, and he
flung himself upward into the darkness.

He stumbled and fell at the top, and crouched for
a moment, listening. There were no heavier feet behind him on the stairs, not yet.

His breathing had quickened a little, but not so much as Derek's. He could hear it, ragged, rasping, from the lower hallway.

"It won't do you any good, Robbie. You can't get away."

Robbie made a rude suggestion. He wasn't wholly sure what it meant, but he knew it was the ultimate in rude suggestions.

"We need to talk, Robbie."

"So talk," Rob said. Derek sounded in worse physical condition than he ought to be at his age. Old Max could run pretty good; he'd raced Rob and beat him a couple of weeks ago. Old Max . . . not guilty at all, and he and Teddi could have been trusted, if he'd only known. Then he wouldn't be in this predicament.

"What's your evidence? What have you got?"

Rob laughed.

He wouldn't have thought it possible, that he could laugh under such circumstances.

"Look, kid, you can make this easy or tough. It's up to you."

"Easy or tough for you, you mean? What do I care how tough it is for you?"

"You know I can't let you tell anybody about me." The voice rose up the stairway. By straining his eyes Rob could make out what he thought was a figure, but the front hallway was very dim. At least Derek couldn't get at him unexpectedly. The stairs would creak the minute he set foot on them.

"I won't have to," Rob said, hoping he sounded more assured than he felt. "I told you, I hid the evidence. They may not find it tonight . . . but they will tomorrow, or the next day." He was only exaggerating by a week or so. Or maybe if he died tonight, if Derek killed him or they just couldn't find him, they'd postpone the wedding, after all. They wouldn't want a wedding and a funeral all at once, would they? He was amazed that he could think of it so calmly.

"You're lying, Robbie. You don't have any evidence. I didn't leave any."

"That's what they all think. What did you come back here for, if not to check? You didn't know I was here."

"No," Derek confessed. "But there's nothing here to indicate to anybody that I pushed Aunt Bea out the window. And nobody else is going to know where I got the cat scratches. By the time I put on a short-sleeved shirt again they'll be healed up, and nobody will ever know anything about them."

"So why did you come back?"

Derek's breathing was less ragged; he was catching his breath. "All right. I'll admit I came back to pick up the empty shells. I suppose you found them."

"Yes."

"They won't do you any good. The police will never see them."

"They know I said somebody was trying to kill me. They might not have believed me then, but they will if I turn up dead or missing. They'll keep looking until they find you."

"Oh, I don't think so." Derek was regaining his confidence. "Everybody who's ever been in this place knows what a firetrap it is. All those crappy newspapers everywhere."

"Nobody ever came to see her."

"Not to visit, no. But the meter readers came, and the paper boy, and the milkman, and the mailman. Everybody who ever looked in the door or a window knows what it's like. And there's this crazy kid with a bunch of wild ideas, afraid of being punished for making up lies and stirring up trouble, he comes over here and hides and he manages to burn the place down. That's an accident, that's not anything to hold anybody responsible for. They got no reason to come looking for me."

"They will have, when they find the chicken."

He wasn't sure he'd meant to say that; he couldn't judge if he'd been smart or stupid. For a few seconds Derek didn't say anything.

"What do you mean?"

"I mean I hid it, with a note saying why, and where it came from, and what's the matter with it." He lied boldly, willing Derek to believe him.

He heaved a quick breath below. "How did you know about the chicken? Did it taste funny? I didn't think it would."

Rob was silent. The more Derek had to worry about, the better.

"Where did you hide it?"

Rob cocked his head, listening. Another car . . . but this one, too, kept right on going. No, it was stopping, it was pulling up right in front of the house . . .

Derek heard it, too. The shadows at the foot of the stairs moved, blurred, stilled.

"It's Max. Coming back from the rehearsal. And Steve and Darcy, too."

Was there any chance they'd hear him if he yelled?

"Go ahead," Derek invited, reading his thoughts. "But you'd better make it a good one the first time, because I'll strangle you before you get out a second yell."

"How you going to make that look accidental?" Rob demanded. He was pretty sure they wouldn't hear him, anyway. Their voices reached him, faintly. Doors slammed.

"When they find your body in a burned-down house, it will be hard to tell you were throttled first. I've wanted to throttle you for years, you know."

"Why? What for?"

"Always sitting around somewhere, quiet, listening. Behind the couch, up that damned tree, in the bushes alongside the porch. I'd have got a lot further with Darcy if you hadn't always been underfoot, popping up at awkward moments. Nosy little bastard."

"I couldn't help it if you came along and sat down next to where I was." Had they all gone into the house next door already? He couldn't hear them anymore. Maybe he should have tried to yell, maybe he should have run to that window in the front bedroom, which could be opened easily, and called before they got inside. Derek wouldn't have dared do anything once he'd got their attention, would he?

But it was dark enough now so that he couldn't have run directly to it, and getting lost wouldn't have helped much. He tried to remember which door it was, the second or the third?

"What are you doing?"

The demand startled him; he'd been quiet too long. "Nothing."

153

"There's nothing you can do, you know. No way you can get away from me."

Rob was aware of his dry mouth and his moist palms. The heat lingered in the upper floor of the old house. He wondered if he could move more quietly if he took off his shoes, then decided that they were rubber-soled and probably as quiet as his sock feet would be. He tried to remember the layout of the house, from the outside. Was there anywhere a roof that he might drop to, a way to climb down?

He couldn't remember anything. It was a tall house, very high off the ground, with the second-floor level way above the same story in his own house. There was lots of fancy scrollwork and knobs and curlicues, but he didn't think any of it offered hand or footholds. There was no lower-roofed room like the Mallory service porch, either. If he went out any of these windows it would kill him, sure.

It might well kill him to stay in here, too.

Was Derek serious? Did he intend to burn the house? But if he tried to burn it now, before everyone in the neighborhood went to sleep, there was a good chance somebody would see the fire and call the fire department before it got very far. In spite of the newspapers, Rob didn't think it would burn to the ground in a few minutes.

Still, if he were on the inside, helpless . . . and Derek would see to it that he *was* helpless . . . it might burn enough to do what Derek wanted.

He heard another car. This time, when Derek moved to peer out the glass panes of the front door, he didn't say anything. Rob felt the pounding start in his throat. Was it his father finally coming home?

He had to know. He couldn't stand not knowing. He rose silently from his crouching position, moving toward what he thought was the room from which he had been fired upon.

"Rob?" The voice from the depths of the house was sharp, demanding.

He didn't wait, but opened the first door he encountered that was on the right side of the house.

It wasn't the same room . . . there was furniture in it. The streetlight allowed enough illumination to enable him to avoid the bed, and he reached the window as Derek again called, "Robbie?"

He thought it was his father's car at the front curb, but it was parked ahead of Steve's Mustang, and he couldn't see enough of it to be sure. Somehow it gave him hope, though, just to think that his father had returned. Even if he couldn't think of any way to contact him. His father was there. He was available, only a short distance away.

He heard Derek starting up the stairs. He was coming slowly, cautiously. He must know something Rob didn't know about how to climb the stairs, because he wasn't making as much noise as Rob had, but he couldn't help being heard.

Rob tugged helplessly at the window, finding it sealed. There wasn't time to search for anything to break it with. He moved back toward the hallway, afraid of being trapped in this room with no exit and no open window.

The stool was so low he didn't see it, but he didn't pause to moan about the bruises it made on his legs.

He scooped it up and ran with it, careless now of sound, flinging the stool as hard as he could down the stairs.

Derek was still far enough down to be caught in the face and chest, and he wasn't expecting it.

He fell backward, swearing, tangling again with the stool before he could bring himself to a stop.

"That kind of thing won't get you anywhere, Robbie. I didn't want to hurt you, but you're making me mad."

Rob said nothing. He had learned that he could move about much more quietly than Derek. Maybe Derek knew the house better . . . and again, maybe he'd never been up here before this afternoon, either . . . but right this minute he couldn't be sure where Rob was.

Again Derek started up, again slowly, but Rob didn't have anything more to throw. He began to edge away, toward the front of the house, trying not to make any sound at all. He went into the first bedroom he came to, on the opposite side of the hall from the rooms where he'd been before. Maybe Derek would look for him in the wrong place, maybe he'd turn his back long enough so Rob could slip past him and get back down the stairs . . .

It wasn't totally dark in any of the upper rooms that faced the street, because of the streetlights. They didn't show much, but enough so that Rob could move without fear of maiming himself, unless there were more low stools.

Miraculously, the door opened without sound. The heat was more intense here; the room faced the west

156

and had taken the brunt of the afternoon sun, and the smell of dust and mildew were strong.

He didn't close the door because he wanted to see where Derek went and try to get past him. The interior hall, however, was much darker than the rooms themselves. He wasn't sure he could see anything.

Rob paused just inside the room, uncertain what to do next.

The house was on the corner, and there were houses directly across the street both north and west, but he didn't think he could make anyone hear him if he got a window open and yelled. The Dunbartons lived in one of the houses, and they'd already gone to bed, or were out, because there were no lights. In the other direction, the Millers had their entire house lit up, but he knew they always played a couple of TVs and a stereo.

Derek had reached the top of the stairs. Rob heard a board creak and stopped breathing. There was a clicking sound; it took Rob a moment, until Derek swore under his breath, to realize he'd tried a light switch and found that it didn't work.

"You might as well come out, Rob. You can't get away."

Rob began to inch across the room. If he could get behind something, so that he wouldn't be seen unless Derek came all the way into the room, he had a better chance. Not that Rob thought his chances were very good, no matter what he did. All the advantages seemed to be on Derek's side. But as long as he was still living, there was reason to try.

He bumped into a bed. Dust rose in nose-tickling

clouds. The bed seemed very high; Rob bent over to see if it was really so much further off the floor than usual, if there was room to get underneath it.

Out in the hall Derek was mouthing obscenities. Rob scarcely heard them, wriggling under the old-fashioned bed, concentrating on not bumping anything that would produce a sound. He had to take the jar of spiders out of his pocket, and he held it, slippery with the sweat from his palm.

A car moved in the street below, slowly, then passed by; Rob heard it without thinking about it, straining to hear any sound Derek might make.

The click of another light switch carried clearly to him, and a band of pale light appeared. Derek had found a bulb that still worked.

This seemed to give him more confidence. He moved along the hall, opening doors one after the other, making no secret of his whereabouts.

He hopes he's going to scare me so bad I won't be able to think, Rob decided. *Well, to heck with you, Derek.*

He was getting awfully uncomfortable; he had to go to the bathroom, and it kept him from concentrating on his escape. Still, the fact that he wasn't witless with fear was good, in a way.

Derek threw open yet another door, turned on another light. So far the light was all on the far side of the house, the side facing the Mallory home. Maybe somebody would notice it, especially if they were still looking for him. If they did, somebody'd investigate. There hadn't been a light on the second floor of this house for as long as Rob could remember.

158

Were they still looking for him? Or had they decided he'd run off and was sulking, or hiding from the police? Cripes, what he'd give for a cop right now, he thought, sweat forming on his face and dust rising in his nostrils from the old carpet.

He felt a fleeting moment of curiosity about the success of his father's mission; had he been able to find Uncle Ray, to do something to keep him out of jail?

Well, even jail was better than being killed by some nut so you couldn't tell that he'd pushed his aunt out the window. If the police were looking for him because they were mad about him making what they thought was a crank phone call, what was the worst they would do to him when they caught up with him?

He didn't remember ever seeing a movie about just exactly his own problem. There had been one about a man who made obscene phone calls. They didn't tell what the guy actually said, which seemed like a cop-out, but when they caught the caller they sent him to jail. He must have said something really terrible to the ladies he called, and Rob had been very disappointed not to learn what it was.

Still, he hadn't done *that*, and besides, he thought now he could prove what he said was true. They might arrest him right at first, but his father would get it all straightened out. The District Attorney was an officer in the Lions Club, the same as his father, and they both played golf when they got a chance. They wouldn't railroad him into any jail term, not when they found out the truth about Derek.

The door of the room he was in was flung back

159

against the wall so hard that something fell . . . maybe a picture off the wall, maybe some plaster. Rob was unable to keep from jerking at the sound.

"Where are you, you crummy little runt?"

In the movies that was sometimes good, when the bad guy got so mad and shook-up he didn't reason logically anymore. To Rob it seemed coldly terrifying, because now he could believe that Derek meant what he said; he intended to kill Rob if he had to destroy the house to do it.

He could see Derek's feet; he wore size twelve sneakers, tan ones, and yellow socks. The wall switch crackled, but the light did not go on.

"All right," Derek said in a low, deadly voice. "You want to make it difficult, we'll play it that way. And it's too late now to get any sympathy from me. I'm going to get you any way I can, boy."

He turned, going away, feet sounding heavily as he moved toward the stairs. He'd turned out the lights as he passed the open rooms, so if nobody had noticed them they wouldn't now.

Rob listened, not trusting his senses that said Derek was going downstairs. Yet how could he make those sounds on the stairs unless he really did go?

In the silence that followed Rob lay for a little longer, listening. There went that same car . . . he could tell it was the same one because there was a slight miss in the engine. Hadn't it been around the block a couple of times already? It stopped, and he could hear nothing at all.

Had Derek gone downstairs? All the way? Was he waiting down there now, listening, ready to pounce if Rob came out?

He didn't know, but he couldn't stay under the bed. If Derek set the house afire, the second floor was no place to be.

Slowly he began to inch his way out, not forward, toward the still-open door, but backward, just in case it was a trick and Derek would suddenly turn on a light and catch him halfway out, helpless.

He was free, and nothing had happened. He got slowly to his feet, his eyes quite used to the dark now. He was standing near a window that looked down on the side street, and he glanced down.

There was a car at the edge of the street. Hardly anybody ever parked there, because Mrs. Calloway always raised cain when anyone used what she considered her part of the curb.

A light glowed, briefly, through the windshield, and went out: the red pinprick of a cigarette.

There was someone down there, someone who might help him if he could contact them.

Rob pushed aside the lace curtains, inhaling more dust, and tugged at the window, but it didn't move. His fingers found the catch and twisted it easily enough, so it wasn't locked. The blamed thing was painted shut, and he had nothing to chip away the paint. And no time to do it, anyway. If he started anything that made any noise, old Derek would be down on him like S.O.B. on a helpless sparrow.

If he broke the window . . . which was unlikely unless he could find something small enough and heavy enough to throw through it . . . and the person below didn't respond immediately . . . Derek would know at once where he was and decide that waiting for a fire to consume him was too slow. As he'd pointed out, if they found Rob's burned body they wouldn't know whether he'd been strangled first or not.

Below, on the street side of the car, the door opened and a man got out. Rob caught his breath. It was darker here than on Saraday Street, but what light there was caught the glint of a badge on the man's chest.

A cop. The cops were out there. Still looking for *him*? Cripes, he had to find some way to attract attention . . .

He groped around the room, trying to find something . . . anything . . . loose enough to pick up, a chair leg might do it . . .

There was no chair in the room. Only the bed and a dresser that must have weighed two hundred pounds. All right, then, before the cop was gone, he'd try sticking his fist through the window. Maybe he'd cut himself all up, and take a chance on bleeding to death, but he didn't think it was as painful to bleed as it was to burn.

Maybe, he thought, hesitating a moment longer, he could stick his foot through it, instead. His tennis shoes might offer some protection from the breaking glass. The cop was still down there, smoking the last of his cigarette, just standing there. He wasn't paying any attention to Mrs. Calloway's house.

The trouble with kicking was that the window was so high off the ground.

It was then that he heard the sounds from the lower floor; frantic scrapings and bangings that indicated frenzied activity on Derek's part.

162

Whatever Derek was doing down there, he was putting everything he had into it. Maybe it would be possible to slip by him, after all, if he was really busy with something. It would be a lot easier than chancing a big cut and maybe bleeding to death by sticking a hand or a foot through a window.

Rob stuck his jar of spiders back into his pocket, further ripping the seam, and stepped to the doorway, straining to hear.

15

He was looking for something.

Rob wasn't sure how he knew that, that Derek was hunting for something. There was the slamming of a door and a muffled curse, making Rob more certain. Money? Maybe the old lady had a treasure hidden somewhere, and Derek hoped to find it before he fired the house. Maybe she had jewels that her nephew knew about.

Rob began to move cautiously toward the head of the stairs. There was a thumping sound, as if a drawer had been jerked all the way out of a dresser and fallen onto the floor.

Derek wasn't thinking about Rob right now, at least not with his full attention. Was there a chance? . . . No, not if he was wandering around, pulling out drawers and stuff.

He remembered that cop outside. Was it a stake-out, did they want Rob bad enough to have cops watching his house for him to come home? He'd thought they only did that with desperate criminals.

Still, he was sure there was at least *one* cop out there. If he knew Mrs. Calloway had died this morning (only this morning?), would he investigate a light in her house if he saw one?

There was some risk in turning on the lights, because Derek might notice and come upstairs. Rob would be more easily captured if the lights were lit. On the other hand, lights could attract the attention of someone who would help him.

So Rob took the time to try all the switches, up and down the hall; he found four that worked.

One of the doors he opened squeaked so badly that he stood with the blood thundering in his ears, wondering if Derek had heard it.

It wasn't another bedroom, however, but a curving stairway.

The tower. It went up into the tower, three tall stories above the street.

His mind raced over the possibilities it offered. Were the tower windows, too, painted shut? Or could they be opened so that he could get out onto the roof?

Only a little of this roof was slanted, as opposed to his own at home. The very top of it was flat and had a little iron railing around it, a captain's walk sort of thing. If he could get onto that . . . he could yell bloody murder and surely someone would hear him . . . Derek wouldn't murder him in cold blood, with help coming on the run, would he?

He had a momentary vision of being shoved off that tremendously high roof, of plunging some forty feet to the ground.

This was followed at once by an even more vivid

image: that of a burning house, with himself trapped above the flames. It was a few seconds before he realized that he could smell smoke.

Had Derek already fired all those newspapers?

Newspapers didn't burn awfully fast, he remembered from trying to dispose of them in the incinerator. Not unless you pulled the pages apart so the air could get between them. So even if something was on fire now, he had a few minutes before it could get up here. If he could get his family, or the cop, to call the fire department, they could rescue him with one of those big ladders . . . he knew they had one that would reach the tower, because he'd seen them use it to paint a church steeple once. Still, his mouth was dry and he wiped sweaty palms on his jeans.

The stairway looked good. He wondered if the light worked up there.

He found the switch; it lit another of the forty-watt bulbs. Mrs. Calloway couldn't have had any money or she wouldn't have been so stingy with the light bulbs, he reasoned.

Rob took a step into the hall below the steps and nudged something with one foot. Pausing, he saw that it was a small packet wrapped in a brown paper bag.

He remembered that Derek had looked into the cupboards in the kitchen, opening a paper bag he saw there. And now it sounded like he was tearing the first floor apart, still looking for something.

Was *this* what he wanted? Something the old witch had hidden?

Unable to restrain his curiosity, even now, Rob picked it up and opened it, holding the bag under the hall light to examine its contents.

This was disappointing, because it seemed to be no more than little packets of some kind. Far too small to be money or jewels or any kind of treasure.

He remembered a show he'd seen on TV a couple of weeks ago. Drugs? Hadn't they packaged drugs something like this?

His breath escaped in an involuntary whistle. Cripes, he'd bet that's why Derek came over here tonight, to find this stuff! Derek hadn't gone into the other room and picked up the .22 shells, although he'd said that was what he came for.

If he burned the house, the shells would vanish, along with the one person who could identify Derek as a murderer. Naturally he wouldn't want to burn up the drugs, if that's what it was, not if he could save them. How much would they be worth, a little bundle like this? Heroin, he knew, was pretty valuable. A million dollars worth, maybe? Boy, what he'd have to tell the guys . . . if he ever got out of here in one piece.

The angry sounds from below had stopped.

Suddenly chilled, Rob realized he hadn't been paying enough attention. Where was Derek?

"Robbie? Hey, Robbie, you hear me?"

Still downstairs, then, but just at the foot of them. The moment Derek put one of his size twelves on the bottom step Rob began to move, easing the squeaking door closed behind him, hoping it would be a few minutes before Derek realized which door it was. He climbed the curving stairs, the paper bag and its contents in his hand.

Why didn't anybody notice anything? That whole houseful of people next door, you'd think one of them would look out the window and realize there were lights in what was supposed to be an empty house, or that the cop would.

He came out into the tower room.

Any other time, he'd have been delighted with it. It was the only part of Mrs. Calloway's house that had ever interested him, but he'd never planned to see it with a killer at his heels. By some miracle, the light here worked, too.

It was a larger room than he'd expected it to be, circular, some fifteen feet in diameter. It had windows all around, with no curtains on them, and the view was so spectacular he wondered why Mrs. Calloway hadn't sat up here even if she did have to climb the stairs.

You could see darned near the whole town, even without binoculars.

Not that it did him any good, because he didn't see any people to yell at. There were lights all over in his own house, and cars in front . . . yes, his father's car was there, too . . . but no people within shouting distance so far as he could tell. Of course if they had any windows open they might hear him, if he could get outside.

The one place he couldn't see was where the police car had been parked, up close to the other side of the Calloway house. Was the cop still there, smoking his cigarette? Would *he* hear if Rob yelled from the tower?

There was nothing in the tower except dust and spiders. Cripes, he could have let his own go and got plenty more spiders up here, he thought. He supposed they'd lock the place up, though, so he wouldn't ever be able to get in here again . . . that is, of course, if he managed to get out of it now.

So far he didn't hear Derek behind him, but it didn't give him any false sense of confidence. It was only a matter of time before Derek figured out where he was, and not much time, at that.

The first window he tried stuck like it was never meant to open, and Rob felt the beginnings of panic. If Derek cornered him here, he was done for.

The second window, after a heart-stopping moment of resistance, opened. He put his head out to look straight down at the front yard below. It didn't make him dizzy, but he knew a fall would kill him. He could yell from here, but then Derek would know where he was . . . and he couldn't be sure the cop was still down there.

Better to open a window where he could get out onto the roof, if he could. Once he was out there, he'd yell, and it would take Derek a few minutes to get to him. If he was brave enough to climb around out on the roof. Lots of grown-ups were really chicken about such things.

This window, then . . . it slid upward with a short creak. Rob looked out, testing the possibilities.

It wouldn't be quite as easy as he'd hoped. He'd have to climb some ten feet on the steeply sloping shingles to reach the flat part of the roof. It hadn't looked that far from below. But if he went straight up from here, Rob saw, if he slipped he'd end up against the base of the tower, not plunging over the edge in a forty-foot drop.

It was then he heard Derek on the stairs.

Only this time he wasn't coming cautiously, he was

running for all he was worth, and Rob didn't have as much time as he needed to get over the sill and onto the slanting roof. He was straddling the sill, one foot in and one out, when Derek burst into the tower room. The door was left open below him, and Rob thought he could smell smoke, stronger now, frightening.

Derek stood panting, staring at him.

"What are you going to do, Robbie? Fly out of the cuckoo's nest?"

"What were you looking for, down there?" Rob countered. "Something in a brown paper bag?"

Derek's expression sharpened, then, taking in the sack on the sill in front of Rob.

"Have you got it? How did you know where it was?"

"Is it worth a lot of money?" Rob demanded. His heart was beating very rapidly, but so long as Derek made no move toward him, he wasn't any more scared than he'd been for the last couple of hours.

Derek licked his lips. "Yes, it's worth quite a bit."

"Is it heroin?"

"Little mister know-it-all today, aren't you, Robbie?"

"I sure never thought my sister would fall for a drug addict . . . even if she did dump him after a while."

Derek's laughter was harsh and unamused. "I'm not *that* stupid . . . I don't use the junk myself."

Rob probed with one sneaker foot at the shingles, testing them for slipperiness. If they were, too bad, he was going to have a devil of a time getting up them. "But you were stupid enough to let Mrs. Calloway know you had the stuff."

A dull flush swept over Derek's face. "The old bat.

I had to have someplace to hide it . . . just for a couple of days. So I thought under her porch was a reasonable place; I never saw her on her front porch, before, let alone looking *under* it."

"But she found it," Rob reasoned. "And when you wanted it back, she wouldn't let you have it."

"The old witch. That's all I needed, to get caught with . . . my scholarship, my job . . . it was bad enough losing Darcy, but I couldn't . . . I tried to reason with *her,* but there *wasn't* any reasoning with her! And all this talking isn't going to do you any good, either, Robbie, my friend, because the more you know the more important it is to shut you up."

"Maybe the fire will keep you from getting out, too," Rob pointed out. He shifted his weight slightly, ready now to swing the other leg over the sill. He didn't think Derek was brave enough to follow him up the roof, but you never could tell. Desperate men did desperate things, and Derek was desperate, all right.

Derek gave another of those croaking barks that passed for laughter. "It's not easy to start a fire without using gas or kerosine or something, even all those damned papers don't want to burn . . . No, now that you've led me up here maybe this is a better idea. You'll just fall out the window and break your stupid neck. Give me the bag."

Rob stared at him. Why should Derek think he would do anything he didn't have to do? If he threw the package outside somebody might find it and put two and two together . . .

Suddenly Derek laughed. "Your own fingerprints are on it, Rob! How about that? If you pitch it out, like you're thinking about, they'll find your finger-prints on it! And they'll think that's why you panicked and ran! Not because you saw any murder, but because you were afraid the police would find the bag!"

Rob didn't much care what anybody thought, if they thought it after he was dead. Besides, Mrs. Calloway's prints and Derek's must be on it, too, since they'd both handled it.

In a quick, deft motion Rob picked up the paper bag and threw it. Not to Derek, but toward the open window opposite him, the one that looked straight down to the front yard.

He wasn't first baseman for the Cubs for nothing; it was a clear, hard shot, and it served its purpose. Derek swore, diving to catch the bag, missing it, almost going out the window himself in his efforts.

Rob didn't wait to see what happened; his only interest was in getting out that window, out of Derek's reach. But the motion of throwing with all his strength had put enough strain on his bulging pocket so that the seam ripped the rest of the way, and the jar of spiders popped out.

He grabbed at it, although this was no time to worry about a few spiders. He didn't drop it, though, because he saw Derek's face.

Derek had missed the paper bag, but that wasn't what held his attention at the moment. He could still get out and get the bag before anyone else found it, if he could keep Rob from getting to anyone.

Both of them stared at the other occupants of the tower room, driven out of their home in the light fixture by the heat of the bulb. Spiders, too many to count, fat black bodies bulging and shiny, dropped from the fixture to the floor between the two of them.

Fear rippled across Derek's face, but as the creatures scurried off toward darker corners, he took another step toward Rob.

Rob, for his part, had been brought to a halt, too, but not by fear of the spiders. Two shingles had broken loose when he put his full weight on them, and went slithering off over the edge of the roof. If they were all like that, he'd be committing suicide to try to climb them. A quick probe with one rubber-toed sneaker sent another shingle sliding away from him. Rotten. The whole crummy roof was rotten.

He couldn't risk the roof. He knew that now. He might fall through it, he might slide with the loose shingles over the edge, but he didn't have a chance of making it to the top.

He hesitated, fear making his heart pound, while his brain was racing. One hand came up to brace himself on the window frame and he drew it back, quickly, to avoid another of the spiders there.

This was the largest one he'd ever seen. He didn't have any like it in his collection because his mother was scared to death of them.

Derek had seen it, too, and again he hesitated. "This place is full of the things!"

"They're black widows," Rob pointed out, in case Derek didn't recognize the species.

"Are you sure?" Derek seemed hypnotized by the gigantic spider, licking his lips, afraid to come any closer to it.

"Sure. Turn it over, if you don't believe me. There's

a red hourglass spot on its belly. A black widow. They're all black widows. They like places where there aren't too many people around."

What was he going to do? Derek wasn't going to stand off for long because of a few spiders, black widows or not, not when there was a car stopping out front and more voices. If he yelled, if they heard him, would Derek do anything? Would Derek push him out the window and then run, making the people below believe Rob had only yelled as he was falling?

"Their bites are fatal, you know," he said, hoping Derek would hesitate a little longer. If only the people would come around this side of the house, where they could see him . . . surely Derek wouldn't dare push him, then, would he? Why didn't they notice the lights?

Derek's face was pale under the dim bulb, but he swallowed, trying to pull himself together. He knew, as well as Rob did, that he had to act at once or it would be too late to act at all.

Derek was afraid of spiders. Could he make use of that knowledge? Could he gain time . . . just a little time?

The glass jar in his hand was slippery with Rob's sweat. He brought up the other hand and twisted the lid, not looking at the spiders climbing over one another inside it, but watching Derek's face. He'd never actually counted the number of spiders he had, but there were plenty of them. If he could get them all over Derek, shake him up enough to get past him and down those stairs . . .

Derek's expression sharpened. "What are you doing?"

"My dad knew a guy that died because a black widow bit him," Rob said, and threw the jar of spiders.

Derek's harsh cry might have been heard by those below, whoever they were; he dodged and the spiders didn't come out of the jar at all, as Rob had expected. A few of them spilled onto the floor, but Derek made a savage kicking motion that sent the jar spinning across the floor.

"All right, you little creep," Derek said, and his voice was deadly. "Out you go, and see how many bones you can break on the way down!"

For all his fear of spiders, Derek was more afraid of letting Rob escape. He lunged, and even as he yelled for help, Rob did the last thing he could think of.

He swept the gigantic spider off the window frame with his bare hand, flinging it straight into Derek's oncoming face.

16

For a few seconds Derek was a study in horror, the bulging black body a grotesque beauty mark at one corner of his mouth. Even as his frantic hands felt for it, the creature moved, climbing into his thick thatch of dark hair.

"Rob? Rob, is that you?"

He couldn't answer the shout from below, couldn't manage the breath for it. He dove from the windowsill, falling to his knees among the spilled spiders, unaware of them crawling over his outstretched hands. His only thought was to get past Derek, down those stairs . . .

He heard Derek's strangled cry as he beat at his hair, and then Rob was plunging down the stairs, falling, rolling, yelling. Somehow, he'd regained enough wind to do that.

Feet pounded on the lower stairs; when he sprawled full-length in the upper hallway, hands found him, lifted him, and it was a moment before he stopped fighting, realizing that it wasn't Derek, but his father, who held him.

"Rob? Rob, are you hurt?"

Behind him, from the tower room, ca... anguish. The police officer behind Walt M... moved toward the stairs.

"It's Derek," Rob said, and wondered why his throat was sore. "He . . . there's a black widow spider in his hair, and he thinks their bites are always fatal. He's . . . pretty dumb about some things."

"Derek?" Mr. Mallory's face seemed more lined, older, than Rob remembered it. "What happened, son?"

"He killed her. Mrs. Calloway. He pushed her out the window because she found some drugs he had and wouldn't give them back to him, I guess."

"Drugs?" That was Fritz, the other cop, coming up the stairs with drawn gun.

"They're in a sack out on the lawn; I threw them out the window."

He was tired, so tired his legs were trembling, and he still had to go to the bathroom.

"What were you doing over here? Didn't you know everybody was looking for you?" his father demanded.

"The police were going to arrest me, weren't they? And I had to hide until you came home. Only Derek found me."

"You saw him push Mrs. Calloway out of the window? Why didn't you tell somebody?"

"I think he tried to, Walt." It was Fritz, the redheaded one. "Not once, but half a dozen times, from what we've been able to gather. Even called the police, but until we'd done some investigating it didn't seem very likely. He hung up before we could get any real information, and then hid when we came to the

He raised his voice. "You need any help up there, Riley?"

"No. He's coming down under his own steam," was the shouted reply.

Rob turned quickly away. He didn't want to see Derek. Not ever again, if he could help it. "I want to go home," he said.

"Sure, son. There's a lot we need to know; we'll want to ask you some questions," Fritz said.

He felt awfully tired, and if he didn't get to a bathroom pretty soon he was going to embarrass everybody by wetting his pants. His father and Fritz laughed when he told them.

"We're not in that much of a hurry, son. You go ahead; I'll be along in a minute," Fritz assured him.

They were coming down the stairs, Derek and Riley. Rob moved quickly to the other stairway, leading down into the sad old house. "I'm hungry, too. Starved. Can I have a peanut butter sandwich before I answer questions?"

"Yes, sure." Mr. Mallory kept a hand on Rob's shoulder. It was a big, warm, heavy hand. It felt good.

Rob cleared his throat.

"Dad."

"Yes, son?"

"Am I . . . under arrest or anything?"

"No. No, I don't think you're under arrest, or anything," his father said, and he sounded so odd that Rob looked up at him, wondering what was the matter.

"I guess I messed up the wedding plans, didn't I?"

"No more than anybody else did," Mr. Mallory said with a sigh as they started down the second flight of stairs.

Rob remembered then. "Is he going to go to jail? Uncle Ray?"

"No. He's just going to work his tail off, paying back the money he took. It may be the best thing that ever happened to him."

Rob felt worn out, drained. "What . . . what will they do with Derek?"

"I don't know, son. It's hard to believe he . . . well, I guess you can have a boy in your house off and on for years and not really know anything about him. The police will take care of Derek."

The smell of burned paper was strong in the lower part of the house, and there was a little smoke, but not much. Mr. Mallory headed toward the front door, but Rob held back.

"No . . . I'd rather go out the other way." He didn't want to walk out into the midst of the crowd he knew was there; he didn't want to answer all *their* questions.

"The back door's hard to get to; there was a pretty good fire going in the kitchen," his father said gently.

"Is it all right if I go out the window, then? The same way I came in?"

They didn't say anything when Rob pushed aside the lace curtains and climbed out into the tree. He balanced for a minute in the very heart of it, wishing he could just stay there for a few hours until everything had died down.

He wondered if it would ever be the same, if the cherry tree would ever again feel as safe and as comfortable as it had before, or if he'd always remember this one day and the things he had seen from these branches.

He heard his mother's voice and knew she'd been crying. "Wally? Where's Robbie? Is he all right?"

"He's fine, honey. Just fine. Give him a few minutes in the tree and he'll come down. He's hungry. He wants a peanut butter sandwich."

There were people all over the place, filling the yard, spilling out onto the sidewalks. There were three fire trucks, unreeling their hoses, running them into the house.

His cousin, Annabel, stood unsuspecting beneath the tree. He had a moment's regret that the spiders had all been turned loose up there in the tower. That would have given her something to remember him by.

"Come on," Mr. Mallory's voice rose above the others. "All my crew, back into the house. We've got a wedding coming off tomorrow, and we're not going to let any of this spoil it."

Rob sat a moment longer, relieving himself into Mrs. Calloway's flower bed. It wasn't a gesture of disrespect, it just seemed quicker and easier than forcing his way through that crowd inside to get to a bathroom.

S.O.B. came bounding across the lawn as Rob slid out of the tree; the cat made a little cry and pushed against Rob's ankles.

Rob scooped him up, rubbing his cheek against the thick black fur. He walked toward the house, slowly, stroking the cat.

They were taking Derek away; he could hear the sounds of the police radio and see the red lights flashing. He felt very strange about Derek. He didn't ever want to see him again, and once he'd told the police all he knew, he didn't want to talk about him anymore, either; but he knew he'd never forget him.

He went up the back steps and into the house.

There was still that blamed wedding to get through.

WILLO DAVIS ROBERTS

Willo Davis Roberts was born in Grand Rapids, Michigan and spent her childhood summers on the shores of Lake Michigan and Grand Traverse Bay, then, later, Grand Marais on the southern shore of Lake Superior where her father operated a sport trolling boat.

She now lives in Eureka, California with her husband, David, two of their four children and an Airedale named Rudy, in a Victorian gingerbread house that was built in 1880. She has an extensive library and relaxes by playing the organ.

Mrs. Roberts has had approximately forty books published, most of them gothics, suspense and medical background novels for adults. This is her first book for children.